D0176976

DAD
DROID

With special thanks to:

Clare Blakeley
Halinka McTaggart

Chris Bran & Justin Chubb

Illustrated by Justin Chubb

This edition first published in 2019

Unbound

6th Floor Mutual House, 70 Conduit Street, London W1S 2GF

www.unbound.com

Text Design by PDQ

A CIP record for this book is available from the British Library

ISBN 978-1-78352-730-4 (trade pbk)
ISBN 978-1-78352-732-8 (ebook)
ISBN 978-1-78352-731-1 (limited edition)

Printed in Great Britain by CPI (UK) Ltd.

To our dads, Tony and John

CONTENTS

1

A FUR COAT AND TWO ODD SHOES

'Why do you always walk on the other side of the street to your dad?' Minnie asked in her high, sing-songy voice, which sounded exactly like a small ginger-haired girl with glasses who lived next door (which is what she was).

Freddy glanced across to where a lanky man in a ladies' fake fur coat was striding down the pavement opposite, lifting his legs like a deranged horse.

'Because I don't want to be seen with him. He's *so* embarrassing,' said Freddy. He straightened his school blazer, which was very clean and neat.

Everything about Freddy Bird was clean and neat. His blond hair was cut perfectly straight across his forehead. Even the mole on his chin was precisely in the middle. Something struck his cheek. Minnie was picking bits off an eraser and pinging them at him as they walked along.

'Why's he wearing different-coloured shoes?' she went on, nodding towards Freddy's dad.

'I don't know.'

'What's he doing with his legs?'

'I don't know.'

'Why has he just walked into that lamp post?'

All these were valid questions. Freddy turned to Minnie to explain but as he did so his dad leaned round the lamp post he'd just collided with and shouted: 'Wait, Freddy! I haven't given you a KISS!'

Freddy tried to ignore him, going bright red, and hurried on. He could see his classmates in the playground, so he sped up to try and dart through the gates before his dad could catch him up.

But it was too late. Before Freddy could stop him, his dad had scooped him off his feet and began spinning him faster and faster in a circle. Freddy's legs flashed through the air like some sort of crazed human turbine. His dad's bristly chin felt like sandpaper against his cheek as he gave him a horrid sloppy kiss. He always did this sort of thing in front of people – like Freddy was some sort of stupid baby.

'DAD! STOP IT! PUT ME DOWN! EVERYONE'S LOOKING!'

By now his entire class was watching. 'Faster! Spin him faster!' they shouted.

Soon the pair had built up such momentum that they spun out of control, crashing into the statue of the school cormorant and knocking over two teaching assistants, before coming to rest on a pile of old cardboard and sticky tape (which was a sculpture by the Year 3s intended to symbolise 'Hope', but which actually symbolised the fact that none of the Year 3s were any good at sculpture).

Freddy looked up from the heap. Miss Arbourteel, his French teacher, was standing over them, pursing her lips in disapproval.

'I wish you would act your age,' she said coldly.

'Sorry, Miss,' said Freddy, getting to his feet.

'Not *you*,' she said, and pointed a long chilly finger at his father, '*him*.'

Miss Arbourteel was tall and pretty. She wore tailored jackets and skirts with lots of buttons and had her hair scraped back in a bun.

Freddy's dad stood up and bowed, theatrically. The sleeve of his coat brushed Miss Arbourteel's dainty shoes.

'*Pardon, mon petit cham-pig-non*,' he said, in a terrible French accent.

Miss Arbourteel rolled her eyes, turned on her heel and headed back into the school building.

'You just called her a little mushroom!' Freddy said, straightening his uniform.

'Did I? My French is a bit rusty these days.'

As the school bell rang, Freddy hurried inside, too annoyed to look back, aware that his dad was now waving goodbye and shouting: 'I couldn't find any tuna so you've got icing sugar and sweetcorn in your sandwiches!'

*

As he settled down to his first lesson – which coincidentally was French with Miss Arbourteel – Freddy glanced out of the classroom window. He could see his dad in the far distance, heading up the big hill that overlooked the town. He was still walking in the same ridiculous manner, except now he seemed to be going even faster, his legs moving in opposite directions like a newborn foal trying to stand up on an ice rink.

As Miss Arbourteel approached, handing out exercise books, she paused and followed Freddy's eyeline out of the window, in time to see his dad crash through a hedge into a field of cows.

She tutted and shook her head as she marched to the front of the class.

*

Freddy's dad – or 'Bert' as he was known to most people – actually had a good reason for his outfit and strange walk. He was an inventor who worked at Wortnall's, a local company that produced all kinds of amazing gadgets.

Bert was wearing different-coloured shoes because the yellow one on his left foot was actually the prototype of the *Automated Ladies' Leg-Lift*, a device he was working on to help posh, lazy women in high society walk long distances with the minimum of effort. The shoe sent regular pulses of high voltage to the knee, triggering a reflex action, so your leg suddenly sprang up with the electric shock. The resulting movement wasn't exactly walking; it was more of an uncontrolled spring or hop.

But then it *was* only a prototype.

The fur coat had nothing to do with this invention. It was just the first thing Bert had grabbed on his way out and had once belonged to Freddy's mum.

Bert's inventions could be seen throughout the town and had revolutionised people's lives. For instance, there was the *Hair-Razor*. Positioned on street corners, this was a small metal booth you sat in to have an automated haircut at a very reasonable price. After placing your coins in a slot, you pressed buttons to select one of a range of hairstyles. Then a helmet lowered over your head and a series of intricate scissors, tongs and curlers whirred into action. After just seven seconds, when the helmet lifted off, your hair had been trimmed, washed and perfectly blow-dried (with a range of optional finishing touches like gel, spray or wax).

Currently, there was a choice of three different styles:

Crabcakes
Mr Frizz
and
The Lola-Fringe

These were all highly distinctive and attracted a lot of attention at first. But now the whole town was using the *Hair-Razor*, and everyone had got used to them.

Whilst *Crabcakes* and *Mr Frizz* were favourites with the men, *The Lola-Fringe* was mainly chosen by women; although after short-sighted Mr Wilkins from the library accidentally pressed the wrong button, he started a new trend amongst the elderly male population for huge glossy domes encircled by a fringe of delicate curls. In fact, the 'Lola Men' as they came to be known, became a recognisable feature of the town, often to be seen hanging round street corners in unthreatening gangs, playing cards or smoking pipes, the wind toying gently with their fringes.

The only downside of the *Hair-Razor* was that since its introduction all the hairdressers and barbers in the town had gone out of business. Now they wanted revenge and had started creeping out at night to prune everyone's trees and hedges into a variety of increasingly complex haircuts, to demonstrate how much better they were than those 'metal snipping boxes'. For Freddy the situation was about to take a more sinister turn.

After school Freddy and Minnie made their way home through the winding backstreets of the town. To Freddy's

annoyance, Minnie had decided to be a robot and was wearing a cardboard box on her head and making him give her directions.

'Left a bit, right a bit,' he said in a bored voice. 'Now straight. Keep going. Keep going. Keep going.'

As Minnie kept going, Freddy was suddenly aware of a figure stepping out of the shadows, blocking his path.

He turned to call for Minnie but she was already half-way down the street, walking like a sleepwalker with her arms outstretched, completely sightless under the cardboard box. (She was several streets away before she realised Freddy was no longer with her, and she had to carry on alone, without the box.)

A disgruntled barber, who had once been the owner of the 'Fur and Away' gentlemen's hair salon on the high street, loomed over Freddy, holding a pair of sharp feathering scissors.

'You're that inventor's son, ain't yer?!' he rasped.

'No,' Freddy lied, sensing danger. 'I'm someone completely different.' He racked his brain trying to make up a name. 'I'm... David... Otter... cake.'

'Don't be ridiculous! David's *much* taller than you!' The barber waved his scissors, angrily. 'Your father's *Hair-Razor* has ruined me! I've lost everything! Except my basic styling tools – oh, and my little brush. You know, the one for getting bits of hair off your neck.'

Freddy tried to back away, only to find Mrs Prippard,

once chief stylist at the 'Tong-Tied Hair Academy', standing behind him, brandishing two cans of extra strong-hold hairspray.

'One move and I spray,' she growled.

'No! Please!'

Freddy froze, seeing her scarlet nails poised over the aerosols.

'Yes, he's Bert Bird's boy all right.' She leant down to examine Freddy closer, in a waft of perfume. 'I'm gonna give you a hairdo you'll *never* forget,' she purred. 'Sort of layered round the back with a horrible centre parting – and a little plait on one side.'

Both hairdressers cackled cruelly.

'It's not my dad's fault. Mr Wortnall owns the factory!'

Freddy pointed to the top of the hill overlooking the town, where the grim outline of C. G. Wortnall's factory stood silhouetted against the setting sun.

Mrs Prippard whipped out a pair of styling clippers, which glinted red in the sunset and moved towards Freddy, slicing the blades open and shut.

But before she got a chance to start snipping, the barber grabbed her hand. 'What are you doing? You can't get a layered effect with *those*!' he snapped.

'Yes, I can!' Mrs Prippard sniffed haughtily.

'You can't use a bevelled edge. Not if you want *layers*.'

'What would you know?! I've been cutting hair longer than you!'

The hairdressers completely forgot about Freddy, who stood looking back and forth at them, as though he was watching a tennis match.

'You need a basic *comb* first and a trim with a *low-gauge* scissor!'

'*What?* You're *insane*!'

Freddy took his chance and made a run for it.

He didn't stop running till he got home.

Safe at last, he slammed the front door and leant against it. He'd never been threatened by a hairdresser before and hoped it would never happen again.

*

Freddy's house was a mess of wires, circuit boards and old bits of machinery his dad was working on, so he had to be careful where he trod. Sometimes it took several minutes to even find a chair to sit on and quite often you couldn't open the doors between rooms without hauling some contraption out of the way first. It was years since anyone had seen the downstairs toilet.

Hearing a miaow, Freddy scoured the room for his cat but couldn't see him anywhere amid the junk.

'Timothy? Timmy? Here, boy!' he called.

A sudden buzzing above his head made Freddy duck, as the cat, strapped into a harness underneath a miniature airship, whizzed past, narrowly missing him.

Timmy wasn't looking happy. His little black lips were curled up with a snaggle tooth visible on one side.

'What's Dad been doing to you now?'

As Timmy circled overhead, Freddy caught sight of a notebook lying open on the table, displaying a scrawl of drawings and equations under the title 'Pet-to-Vet Delivery System'.

'Brilliant, isn't it?'

Bert, his dad, walked in holding an old fishing net he'd found under the stairs to catch Timmy with, unaware there was a gaping hole in it larger than a cat.

'It's my new invention to take pets to the vet and back,' he went on. 'I just need to perfect the satnav element. Or as I call it, the "*cat*nav".'

Seeing his dad still in the ladies' fur coat and odd shoes, staring at the cat on the ceiling, Freddy felt a surge of frustration. He rolled his eyes and tutted as he stomped upstairs.

'Freddy?' His dad shouted after him. 'What's the matter?'

But Freddy didn't answer.

Inside his bedroom, which was the only tidy room in the house, with everything neatly folded and arranged along clean lengths of shelving, Freddy sat down and gazed out of his window.

Across the fence, he could see into Minnie's house next door.

In the ordinary dining room, Minnie's ordinary mum was bringing in an ordinary meal, as Minnie's ordinary dad arrived home from his ordinary job. (He owned 'Top Toes Shoe Emporium', one of the biggest shoe shops in town.)

Freddy sighed. More than anything he longed for an ordinary life with an ordinary family, just like Minnie's. Even as he looked out of his bedroom window, a startled-looking Timmy rose into view on the *Pet-to-Vet* airship. With a whir of his tiny propeller, the unfortunate animal sped off.

Freddy's dad hurtled down the road after him, waving the fishing net and calling: 'Press the red button, Timmy! Press the red button!'

But of course Timmy didn't understand. He was just a cat.

2

THE SHARK-CAR

Freddy woke with a start. It was the middle of the night. His clock said 3.39 a.m. and twenty-one seconds.

Twenty-two

Twenty-three

Twenty-four—

He had to force himself to stop looking at it.

Something must have woken him but he wasn't sure what. There was a crash downstairs. He sat bolt upright. Someone was in the house! Maybe a whole gang of hairdressers had broken in to attack him!

Grabbing the torch by his bed, he crept out of his room onto the landing and tiptoed carefully through an obstacle course of bizarre inventions left there by his dad. Reaching the stairs, he accidentally trod on a length of plastic tubing, causing two huge rubber gloves to inflate and grab his ankles (this was his dad's first attempt at a humane trap for badgers). Wrestling himself free, Freddy made his way carefully downstairs.

By the light of his torch he could see a series of black greasy footprints leading from the front door to the kitchen. There was another crash, which sounded like a lot of saucepans clattering to the floor. Heart thumping, Freddy followed the footprints to the kitchen door and pulled it wide open, swinging his light inside. A man covered from head to toe in black oil blinked back in the glare, giving a cry of surprise:

'AAAGH!'

Freddy screamed back: 'AAAGH!' then blurted out: 'Who are you! What do you want?' – and picked up the nearest weapon, which happened to be a feather duster; not the best of defences – unless the burglar was ticklish. Before he could do anything however, the man lunged towards him with a laugh, slithering across the grease-smeared floor.

'It's *me*, Freddy!'

'DAD!' Freddy was half-relieved, half-furious.

'Shut the door quickly! Stop him!' His dad pointed to where Timmy the cat was scampering along the draining board, trying to make a break for it, still attached to the airship by its little harness. The unfortunate creature was now completely bald, glowing with blue-white sparks as he ran.

'Poor Timmy! He crashed into the power lines by the electricity plant, then flew into Mr Hanson's garage and fell in an oil drum,' Bert explained. 'I've been chasing him for miles!'

Reaching the end of the worktop, Timmy sailed through the air and landed by his bowl, sending electricity crackling through it. The smell of cooking cat food and a wisp of steam rose from the bowl. Timmy forgot all about trying to escape and tucked into the delicious snack instead, hovering just above it.

Bert Bird leant forward with interest. 'Incredible. A cat that can *cook food*... Yes... I could call it the *Feline Fryer* or the *Kitty-Cook*!'

'Stop it!' Freddy snapped at his dad, whose eyes looked very large and white in contrast to the rest of his dark oily face. 'Stop inventing things!'

This was the worst thing you could say to an inventor. Bert opened his mouth to answer but was too shocked to think of anything.

'It's half past three in the morning! I've got to be up for school in a few hours!'

Freddy pointed to Timmy's hairless body.

'Look what you've done to our cat!'

'His fur will grow back,' said Bert.

'What about the hairdressers?' Freddy went on. 'They blame you and your *Hair-Razor* thing for putting them out of work. They're really angry with us!'

'But it gives everyone a fantastic multi-layered haircut in seven seconds, in three incredible styles,' his dad gushed.

This was the exact wording on the billboards advertising the *Hair-Razor*, under a photo of some impossibly good-looking supermodels sporting the three different hairstyles.

Bert leant against the cooker but his sleeve was slick with oil and he immediately slid off it onto the floor.

Freddy had had enough.

He stormed up to his room, climbed into bed and pulled the covers over his head. He didn't come out again till his alarm went off.

*

On a normal school day Freddy would get dressed, have breakfast with his dad, then, when the clock in the kitchen said 8.34, they'd collect their bags from hooks by the front door and leave together. But today, instead of going into the kitchen, Freddy just grabbed his bag and left the house on his own.

Hearing the front door slam, Bert – who was sitting at the table idly dismantling an egg timer – jumped to his feet, springs and cogs bursting round him. Freddy was striding along so fast Bert had to run to catch him before he disappeared.

'What are you doing, Freddy?' he called after him.

'Going to school,' Freddy replied, without looking back.

'But I always come with you!'

'I want to go on my own this morning.'

'But you haven't had any breakfast!'

'I'm not hungry.'

Freddy's tummy gave a rumble of protest.

'But you haven't got any sandwiches!'

'I'll get some at school.'

'But you haven't got a coat!'

'It's not raining.'

'But – um – um – um—'

Bert wanted to shout something else parenty but couldn't think of anything. He watched as Freddy turned the corner, nose in the air.

'Oh, well, if that's what he wants.'

Bert shrugged and made his way rather sadly back inside.

*

Walking to school alone for the first time, Freddy noticed lots of things he'd never seen before: the snooty faces of the stone lions on the gateposts of posh Mrs Crumley's house; the missing letters on the sign outside the 'Off Licence' which meant it now said 'O Lice', like the beginning of some poem to a parasite.

Turning a corner, he gazed up at the factory on the hill above the town. A strange fog hung round it, whatever the weather. Not a lovely summer haze or a fresh sea mist, but a murky yellow smoke that clung to the walls, sucking the light and life out of everything. Crows were circling above the factory and perching along cables between its two grim chimneys, like fat inky notes on a line of music.

Wherever you went in town, you could see the outline of the forbidding building. Or rather *it* could see *you*, because it felt like the factory – and the crows that always hung around it – were keeping watch. Apart from the people who worked there, nobody went up to the factory and Mr Wortnall made it clear he didn't like visitors. In fact, in recent years he had built a high wall around it to keep people out.

Freddy hurried on. He was never normally out this early and everywhere seemed strangely quiet and dreamlike. On the street that ran alongside the park, he noticed with a shudder that an oak tree by the entrance had been snipped into a sort of huge, long-layered bob with feathered ends by angry hairdressers. Leaf trimmings on the ground showed it was freshly cut. A short way across the grass a couple of homeless stylists were warming their hands on a pile of burning hair rollers.

Freddy quickened his pace. As he crossed the road, his mind full of worries, he heard a sudden growling sound and looked up to see a car hurtling towards him.

It was going so fast he didn't have time to get out of the way.

With a hiss of brakes and shrieking tyres, the car skidded to a halt millimetres away from him. (It braked so abruptly that a ladybird, which had been clinging to the windscreen, plopped onto the bonnet and rolled off into the road, stunned.)

Freddy – frozen with his mouth open, about to scream – dropped his bag on his foot (which was quite painful, as it was full of big boring books on algebra). He found himself staring into the front radiator of the car, a huge grinning mouth of steel with arching headlights either side, like some weird metallic shark. Hot steam pumped out between the chrome teeth, nearly scalding Freddy's knees in his school shorts.

He recognised the car at once as Mr Wortnall's, although because of its tinted windows he couldn't see who was inside. Usually, you saw it whizzing up the side of the hill towards the factory, catching the sun on its fins, or zooming away from town on important business. Mr Wortnall never mixed with ordinary people and got driven everywhere. No one knew where he came from or anything much about him, but there were rumours that the immense wealth he had built up over the years had turned him into a spiteful, power-crazed man who wanted to take over the town.

Although still in shock, Freddy managed to pick up his bag and start to back away. He had only taken a few steps however when one of the rear windows began to glide down with a squeaking sound. It stopped after a few centimetres and a beady eye appeared in the gap, staring out at Freddy. He heard what sounded like a long drawn-out sigh, then a wisp of yellow-brown cigar smoke, just like the fog around the factory, floated through the gap. Freddy couldn't help spluttering as it coiled round him, smelling like burnt cabbage.

The eye blinked a few times, then a voice asked: 'What is your name?'

Freddy gulped. His throat felt dry. He glanced round, hoping someone might be passing. But the street was empty, sunlight lying in thick slabs along the tarmac. The only sign of life was the ladybird that had just plonked off the car, scuttling away as fast as its six legs could carry it.

'Your *name*, boy,' the voice insisted.

'Er – er – er – Freddy,' Freddy stuttered.

The voice gave a dry laugh without any humour in it and the eye looked Freddy up and down.

'Well, watch where you're walking in future, "Er-er-er-Freddy",' the voice purred. 'I don't want a boy-shaped dent in my car.'

Before Freddy had the chance to reply, the car sped off

impossibly fast, so it was suddenly just a glittering speck, the size of a toy, at the far end of the street. A cloud of acrid cigar smoke hung in the air around Freddy like an afterthought.

His legs felt shaky. He was quivering with fear. None of this would have happened if Dad had been there.

3

LA-DI-DAS AND *SUPERSTACKS*

Three weeks later C. G. Wortnall's newest product was unveiled all over town. As with the *Hair-Razor*, it sprang up suddenly overnight. One morning there they were, gleaming on street corners, having been installed swiftly and silently while everyone was sleeping. The *You-Shoes* was an elaborate vending machine, dispensing a range of new, exciting footwear 'in three amazing styles':

La-di-das
The Gavins
and
Superstacks

The shoes were far more comfortable than anything you could buy in the shops and because they looked so shiny and modern, all other footwear suddenly looked dull in comparison. But the really amazing thing about the *You-Shoes* was that they used technology to actually *help* you *walk*. You just clicked a dial to whichever speed you wanted and off you went: from LIGHT STROLLS to TROTTING, right up to the highest setting – DASH!

Bert's prototype of the *Ladies' Leg-Lift*, which had so embarrassed Freddy, was an early version of the *You-Shoes*, but luckily his dad had been working day and night to improve it – otherwise everyone would be hopping about out of control and throwing themselves through hedges into fields of cows. Billboards appeared overnight with the same supermodels from the poster for the *Hair-Razor*, posing in the three different styles of shoe, with the slogan: *'You-Shoes! The shoe for you and you and you!'*

Stopping in the shadow under one of these huge adverts, Freddy felt a chill creep up his spine. A terrible thought occurred to him: Minnie's father owned one of the biggest shoe shops in town. What would happen to him now?

*

The day the *You-Shoes* arrived, there were queues stretching down the streets. Everybody wanted them and they wanted them NOW.

The bespectacled TV presenter on the local news announced in his nasal voice that the town had come to a grinding halt because so many people had bunked off work to buy them and that there were now mountains of unwanted, ordinary shoes littering the streets, causing accidents and traffic jams.

Freddy got out of school early as the Headteacher suddenly announced an 'urgent staff meeting', which was actually just an excuse for all the teachers to leg it out of the back entrance and join the *You-Shoes*-queues as soon as possible.

Heading home, Freddy passed a couple of businessmen tossing their briefcases merrily in the air and literally springing along in their new *Gavins* – a sculptured ultra-brogue with sleek designer lines and a velvet interior. Further on he had to jump out of the way as a mother with a pram pranced straight at him, laughing for joy as she tested out her *La-di-das* – a swanky high-heel in maroon leather. (He was surprised to see two baby *La-di-das* sticking out of the pram.) Then he had to duck in a doorway as two old ladies dragging tartan wheelie-cases shot past like athletes, wearing *Superstacks* – a platform boot of breath-taking construction with a multi-coloured heel like the layers of a delicious cake.

There was an air of hysteria all over town. People were rushing round trying out the different speeds of each design, bumping into one another. But no one seemed to mind.

Underneath the excitement Freddy sensed something more disturbing. Like people had lost their minds – all because of this new gadget from C. G. Wortnall.

Turning onto his street, Freddy found himself caught up in an unruly mob around the *You-Shoes* vending machine opposite his house. Waiting eagerly at the front of the crowd was short-sighted Mr Wilkins from the library, whose *Lola-Fringe* was looking lovely (though it was always a shock when he turned round and you saw his prune-like features under it). As he stepped off the machine in his *La-di-das* high-heels, everyone realised he'd pressed the wrong button again. Too proud to admit it, he patted his new shoes and said: 'Perfect, just what I wanted,' before setting the little dial on the side of the shoes to CATWALK and strutting off down the street, to stifled giggles.

As Freddy pushed through the crowd, some people pointed at him: 'Look! It's the inventor's son!' 'Let him through!'

Hands reached out and grabbed him, passing him to the front of the queue, where he was lifted up and his old shoes yanked off. Then he was plonked onto the machine, which looked like futuristic weighing scales.

Coins were pushed into a slot and someone pressed a button.

'I don't want any!' Freddy tried to say but the noise of the crowd was too loud and no one heard. The machine fired into action, beaming a network of lasers over his socks, which tickled. Then the contraption started to shake, accompanied by the sweet smell of freshly cut leather. In exactly seven seconds, a pair of *Gavins* were wrapped around Freddy's feet, still steaming – which made them extra nice because there are few things more comforting in life than toasty shoes. He was hoisted off the machine and someone took his place.

Clicking the dial on his *You-Shoes* to the lowest setting, Freddy set off, feeling them lift him in a steady rhythm. He had to admit they did feel good. Like walking in marshmallows on a cloud.

*

'It's baked beans and some of that nice chocolate cake for supper,' Bert said, laying plates in front of them.

Freddy picked up his fork to start then paused, realising his father had served both the baked beans *and* the cake at the same time. He watched as some of the beans trickled off the cake's thick swirly icing.

'Thought it would save washing-up,' said Bert, tucking in. He was jotting something down in one of his notebooks between mouthfuls, on the trail of a new idea.

As Freddy scraped beans off his cake, he caught sight of Timmy drifting past. Although it was a week since his encounter with the electricity cables, none of his fur had grown back and he remained pinkish-grey, occasionally emitting sparks from his bottom. In fact, Freddy's dad had just used him to light the cooker.

'Pass the salt, will you? Or no, the sugar, actually,' Bert said, trying to decide which would best suit his supper. Freddy stood up abruptly to leave the table, his food untouched.

'What's wrong?' his dad asked.

'Nothing,' Freddy fired back.

Bert caught a glimpse of Freddy's shoes. 'Oh you've got some *Gavins*! Comfy, aren't they?'

'Yes, Dad,' Freddy said with a sigh. 'But you know Minnie's dad sells shoes.'

'Does he?'

'Yes, and because of these his shop doesn't stand a chance.'

Bert looked up, his smile fading. For a moment his mind cleared of diagrams and measurements. 'Oh,' he said softly, spooning some more baked beans and chocolate into his mouth.

*

Setting off for school the next day, Freddy saw Minnie on her doorstep being handed her school bag by her mum. Minnie's mum, Mrs Carstairs, had a kind, pretty face. She looked lovelier in her *Lola-Fringe* than anyone else in town and was always very well turned out. He waved at her, but instead of waving back like she usually did, she sent Freddy a look that would have curdled milk, then scurried inside, slamming the door.

'Hi,' he said as Minnie closed her front gate and started walking beside him. She glanced down at Freddy's *Gavins* whirring softly as they carried him along.

'I'm not speaking to you,' she said, as they reached posh Mrs Crumley's lions.

'You *are*,' Freddy observed accurately.

'No, I mean *from now on* I'm not speaking to you.'

They went on a bit more in awkward silence, past the 'O Lice'. All the time Minnie breathed hard through her nostrils, trying to contain her anger. Looking down, he noticed she was still wearing her normal shoes, which looked very curled-up and scruffy next to his sleek *You-Shoes*.

‘What is it, Minnie? Is this about the *You-Shoes*?’

‘Yes!’ She pointed at his *Gavins*. ‘Because of those my dad says he’ll go out of business, just like the hairdressers! We’ll lose everything.’

She sat down on the pavement with tears in her eyes.

‘Look, I’m sorry, Minnie. I didn’t want these things.’ He waggled his *Gavins* at her.

‘Why are you wearing them then?’

‘I got pulled onto the machine and someone threw my old shoes away.’

She grunted. ‘Anyway, my mum and dad told me not to hang around with you any more. I have to find some new friends.’

‘That’s nice.’

At that moment there was a click-clacking from the end of the street. Miss Arbourteel was approaching, on her way to school in her new *La-di-das* (which made a satisfying click-clack when you walked in them). As she drew level with the children, she gestured impatiently: ‘Hurry up! *Vite! Vite!* You will be late!’

Shooting him a sour look, Minnie jumped up and walked with Miss Arbourteel, leaving Freddy to trail after them. His heart felt suddenly heavy. Now even his best friend was angry with him. Freddy wished the factory and Mr C. G. Wortnall would just disappear. Then his dad could get a normal job and everything would be all right.

4

EAR TO EAR

Just as Minnie had predicted, within a week all the shoe shops in town, including her father's, had shut down. Their front windows were soon covered in old newspapers and 'To Let' signs were put up outside.

Forlorn shoe-shop workers could be seen shuffling joblessly about the streets in old-fashioned footwear – anything except *You-Shoes* – which was how you told them apart, because everybody else, without exception, was wearing *Superstacks* or *Gavins* or *La-di-das.*

After the initial shock wore off, just like the hairdressers before them, out-of-work staff from the shoe shops started to leave protests around the town. One morning a pair of pink stilettos was found superglued to the statue in the town square of General Rothwell-Bennett, a serious military figure mounted on horseback. Then a giant promotional boot that had hung for decades above the entrance to 'Stompers Boot Boutique' showed up dangling from the town clock, causing it to stay permanently at five past one.

It turned out Minnie's dad was behind these acts of sabotage, having crumbled under the pressure of losing his Shoe Emporium. The police finally caught him at the zoo, trying to fit two pairs of trainers onto Edgar the anteater (who was a Size 3, with a rather raised instep, it turned out). A mugshot of Mr Carstairs was plastered across the front of the local paper, with the headline: BROUGHT TO HEEL!

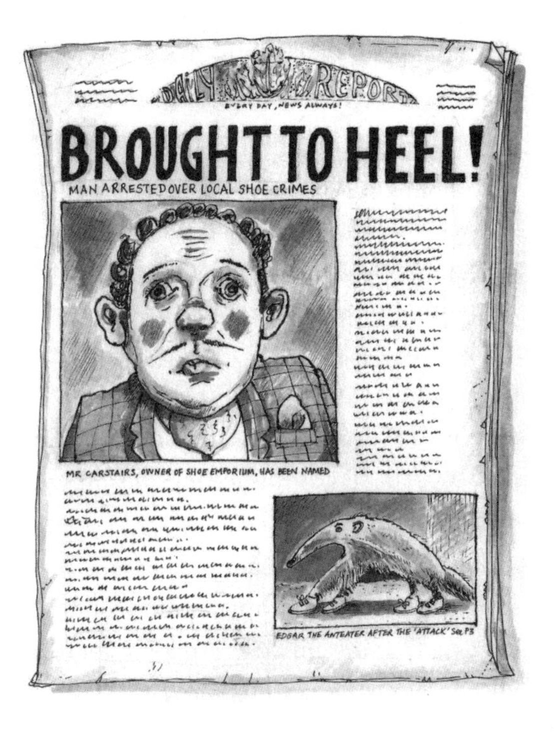

*

At breakfast the next day, Freddy didn't have to say anything to his dad. He just slid the newspaper across to him. Bert murmured quietly, 'Poor man,' and chewed sheepishly on his cereal and toast (in the same bowl).

Minnie didn't come to school that day and the curtains at her house stayed shut. It was as if someone had died.

Later that evening Freddy leaned out of his bedroom window and saw a police car pulling up outside and a rather overweight constable escorting Minnie's father up the drive. Mr Carstairs, normally a dapper man with a small moustache, looked crumpled and defeated as Minnie and her mum came to the door to greet him. He'd been let off with a caution but had been warned not to carry out any further shoe-related crimes. He also had to write a letter of apology to Edgar the anteater (or at least to the zoo), as the poor animal had been left traumatised by the attempted shoe-fitting.

Freddy sat on his bed with a feeling of dread. He felt terrible that his dad was in some way responsible for Mr Carstairs's downfall. It was all getting too much. A loud splosh made him look up.

A piece of paper wrapped around some sort of heavy object had shot through the open widow and landed in the fish tank, narrowing missing Freddy's goldfish, Elvis. When he fished it out, he saw it was a note wrapped round a tin of shoe polish. The paper had got wet and a few of the letters had washed off, so the note now said:

'Sorry I was angry.
Can we be frie s again?
Minnie'

For a moment he imagined Minnie and himself dressed as enormous chips but quickly realised the missing letters were probably an 'n' and a 'd' and she meant 'friends'. As he peered from his window, a second note shot through the air from Minnie's bedroom, directly opposite, thumping him on the head. Her silhouette darted out of sight as her mother came in. The second note, wrapped around a shoe brush, said:

'My parents still won't let me talk to you.'

She had drawn a frowny face underneath.

Remembering a device his dad had been working on, Freddy rooted around in a drawer in the hallway and brought out a pair of plastic ears with speakers fitted into them and tiny microphones in the lobes. These were the *Ear to Ear* communicators.

Downstairs Bert was too busy scrawling calculations on the wall to notice Freddy creeping in and removing Timmy from where he floated asleep.

Back in his room, Freddy fixed the left ear of the *Ear to Ear* communicators onto Timmy, wearing his dad's welding gloves to avoid getting an electric shock from the 'live' cat. Then he opened his window wide and, ignoring Timmy's miaows of protest, gave him a firm push in the direction of Minnie's bedroom. The propeller on the back of the small airship spun frantically as the cat sailed over the fence between the houses.

Minnie was sitting doing her homework when she looked up with some surprise to see Timmy's fat bald face pressed against her window, sparks crackling down his whiskers. What was even more shocking was the large human ear attached to his head. It struck

Minnie that Bert Bird had finally gone too far with his experiments.

To her astonishment the cat seemed to be saying: 'Minnie! Minnie! Open the window!' in an urgent voice. When she pulled up the sash, however, she found the voice was coming from the ear, which was plastic and detachable.

'Hi, it's me!' Freddy was saying out of it. 'Can you hear me, Minnie?'

'Yes,' she said into the ear. 'Loud and clear.'

'This way we can still talk to each other without your mum and dad finding out,' said Freddy. 'Oh, but don't touch the cat with your bare hands, you might get an electric shock.'

Using an old wooden tennis racquet, Minnie gently tapped the ear off Timmy, then gently batted him round the right way and gave him a firm shove to send him back. Unfortunately, she misjudged the angle and he went whizzing past Freddy's house into a pair of extra large Y-fronts hanging on old Mr Trimming's washing line, three houses down.

Minnie crouched, whispering into the ear so her mum and dad wouldn't hear her. 'It's horrible here now. My parents keep arguing. My dad says we'll have to sell the house.'

'No! That's terrible! Where will you go?'

'I don't know. That's what most of the arguing's about.'

'I got your note, Minnie. I'm so pleased you want us to be *fries* again.'

'What?'

'Listen, I've decided to go up to the factory after school tomorrow and speak to Mr Wortnall.'

Minnie gasped. 'Won't it be dangerous?'

'I don't care.'

'What are you going to say?'

'I don't know yet. But someone's got to stand up to him.'

'Well, I'm coming too!' There was silence from the ear. 'Freddy? Freddy? Are you there?'

Freddy's bedroom door swung open. He thrust the ear under his pillow as his dad came in.

'Who were you talking to?'

'No one. Just... practising my French.'

'Come on, it's getting late. Hop into bed.'

Freddy climbed under the covers. Bert clicked off the light and sat next to him.

'Look, Fred, I'm sorry about everything. I didn't mean to upset you.'

Freddy took his hand.

'But what are you working on now, Dad? What's Wortnall going to do next?'

For the first time Freddy noticed panic in his father's eyes and deep wrinkles on his forehead.

'I can't tell you, Fred. I'm sworn to secrecy.' He looked round uneasily, as if they might be being spied on.

Wortnall's beady eye flashed into Freddy's mind, glaring at him from the shark-car.

'Anyway go to sleep,' his dad said, tucking him in and giving him a bristly kiss.

But no matter how he tried, Freddy couldn't get to sleep. As he lay in the moonlight, watching Elvis swimming round and round, he couldn't stop thinking about Wortnall and Minnie's angry parents and the panic in his dad's eyes.

5

CROWBOTS

Next day, all through the last lesson, which was Double French, Freddy scribbled plans in his jotter for his visit to the factory. He had begun writing a speech, which in his mind was a dramatic plea set to orchestral music that would convince Wortnall to pack up his factory and leave town. So far he had written three words: 'Dear Mr Wortnall', and drawn a picture of a rabbit, a man with big teeth and some clouds.

Meanwhile at the front, Miss Arbourteel was perched on the edge of her desk, swinging her *La-di-das* as she took the class. As usual the comprehension piece she had set them was about a young girl called Chantelle who seemed to be a lot like Miss Arbourteel, and a tall man with '*le cheveux brun*' (brown hair) called Jerome who brought her '*les chocolats*' *et* '*les fleures*' (chockies and flowers) and who had gone suddenly to Belgium to work as a doctor. The French phrases she dictated to the class were often interspersed with sighs and dabs of a handkerchief to her eyes.

She was in the middle of all this when she broke off suddenly and shouted, 'Freddy, *attention s'il vous plaît!*'

Freddy's pen trailed off in the middle of adding a big beard to the toothy man.

'What did I just say?' Miss Arbourteel strode over.

Freddy slammed his jotter shut.

She was glaring at him, her lips twitching. The word 'detention' was forming on them. (Miss Arbourteel was well known for keeping pupils behind after school and making them write endless lines in French about Jerome and Chantelle and their love of small Parisian art galleries.)

'Er... er...' said Freddy.

He had no idea what she had been saying but the last thing he wanted was to be kept in after school when he should be on a mission.

'Jerome and Chantelle,' he began.

'Yes?'

'Were walking?'

'Yes?'

'And then... then...'

Miss Arbourteel moved closer, her top lip curling. 'You were not listening, were you, Frederic!'

'I *was*, Miss! Honestly!'

'Then tell me what Jerome did! Hmm?'

Freddy sighed, racking his brain.

He was about to make a guess when there was a buzz from the top pocket of his blazer and a muffled voice. It was Minnie, speaking from the back of the classroom through the *Ear to Ear* device.

'*Jerome gave her flowers*,' Minnie whispered.

'Jerome ate her flowers,' Freddy said with confidence.

'What?' Miss Arbourteel was shocked. 'Right – detention!'

'*GAVE* her flowers!' Minnie's voice buzzed, louder.

'*GAVE* her flowers, I mean, Miss!' Freddy corrected himself.

'*Oui.* Yes.' Miss Arbourteel suddenly softened. 'Jerome did indeed give Chantelle flowers.' She shook her head slowly, as if remembering something, and her eyes misted over. 'But the flowers withered and died in the vase of my mother – I mean, *Chantelle*'s mother.' She stared into the middle distance. 'And then,' she said in a somewhat bitter voice, 'Jerome went to Belgium...'

A tear welled in her eye.

The bell rang. Time to go. Freddy leapt up and was first out. Minnie hurried after him. 'Thanks for bailing me out.'

'Don't mention it.' She blinked back at him through her glasses as they crossed the playground. 'Are you still going to see you-know-who?'

'Of course,' he said.

'I'm coming with you.'

'Great!' said Freddy.

Instead of turning left at the school gates to head home as usual, they went right, towards the factory. Minutes later they were passing the last house in town, where a yappy dog lived. As the sound of yapping faded behind them, Minnie gulped and looked ahead to where the road suddenly rose at a steep angle up the hill. Now they were getting nearer, it didn't seem like such a good idea any more.

'Are you sure we should be doing this, Freddy?' she asked a little nervously.

Freddy stopped in his tracks and fixed her with a stare. 'If you're scared, go back. I'll go on my own.'

'I'm not scared,' she said untruthfully.

'Good. Nor am I,' he lied.

'Good!'

'Good!'

'Good!' Freddy puffed out his chest, striding forward.

Further on they passed the smelly farm, where a black cow peered at them over the hedge, its head turning slowly as it followed their every step, mouth chewing left and right.

The air started to turn murky brown. They were entering the factory fog. The grass on either side looked withered and sickly.

'Stop a minute,' Minnie gasped, out of breath. 'My legs are shorter than yours.' She took off her glasses and rubbed a film of brown dust off the lenses. Looking round, she realised the air was full of the stuff.

'Not far now.' Freddy pointed ahead to where the high walls surrounding the factory loomed on the summit.

They both stopped talking after that because it took all their strength to climb the increasingly steep road and they didn't want to breathe in too much dust. The tarmac gradually ran out, turning into broken gravel. Then a sign appeared out of the fog on a rotting wooden post, which said: 'GO AWAY'.

'That's nice,' said Minnie.

Further on they came to another sign that said: 'DIDN'T YOU SEE THE OTHER SIGN? GO AWAY!' A big ragged crow was crouching on top of it. With a rusty creak it swung its head round and opened its beak wide, letting out a squawk that was so loud Freddy and Minnie had to cover their ears.

'*ARRRRRRK!*'

As they hurried past, Freddy glimpsed wires sticking out of its mouth.

'That's not a real bird!' he whispered to Minnie. 'It's some sort of robot!'

They waded into the long grass away from the road. 'That thing's watching us. Stay down.'

They carried on, trying to keep as low as possible. Above they saw the circling shapes of more crow-things, scanning the area.

A few minutes later they reached the factory. The grass petered out into scorched earth as if the enormous building was some kind of spaceship that had landed there from another planet. As they got closer, they could see the reason for this. There were hundreds of small vents at the bottom of the walls, belching out brown smoke with a hollow blowing sound. It was so hot near the vents it was difficult to stand there long.

Dwarfed by the shadow of the great wall, which ran all the way round the factory, they looked up at its blank expanse towering above them and curving off to either side into the fog. Now they'd reached it, the factory was far larger than they had imagined.

'Where's the door?' asked Minnie.

'It must be here somewhere.'

Keeping to the shadows, where the crow-things were less likely to see them, Freddy and Minnie set off around the vast perimeter wall to look for a way in.

Nineteen minutes and twenty-three seconds later, Minnie said: 'We're back where we started!'

They had come full circle without finding anything.

'Well, that's it,' said Minnie, sitting down.

She brought out a packet of Minty Double-Chockshocks biscuits and put three in her mouth at once.

Freddy was about to sit down next to her, defeated, when he caught sight of something: 'Look! Tyre tracks!'

They followed the grooves left by a set of wheels to where they stopped abruptly at the wall.

'It looks like you can drive in through here. So this *must* open somehow.' He ran his hands over the blank surface.

'What's that?' Minnie said, pointing to a tiny black square in the wall above.

Freddy squinted up. It looked like a small glass tile. 'Maybe it's some sort of button.'

He reached up but even on tiptoe it was too high to reach.

'Oh well,' said Minnie, popping in three more Minty Double-Chockshocks. 'We might (*crunch*) as well (*crunch*) go home (*crunch*).'

But as they turned to go, they saw headlights rising up the hill towards them through the fog.

'It's Wortnall!' cried Freddy, recognising the growl of the shark-car. He pulled Minnie into the greasy undergrowth.

As they peered out, the car's sleek outline came into focus at breakneck speed, screeching to halt a hair's breadth from the factory wall, where the tyre marks stopped.

'Right. I'm going to speak to him,' Freddy said in a shaky voice.

He took a deep breath but didn't go anywhere.

'I'm definitely going in a minute.'

'Go on then,' said Minnie.

'I will.'

'Good!'

'Good!'

But before Freddy had a chance, the roof of the shark-car suddenly peeled open. The back seat rose up on a mechanical arm, lifting a hunched figure in a long black coat towards the button in the wall.

'That's him,' said Freddy. 'That's Mr Wortnall.'

He was operating a joystick, which controlled the crane's movement. First the seat lurched forward, then shot back, then tipped a bit.

'For someone who creates amazing gadgets, he's not very good with them,' Minnie said.

After a series of ungainly jolts in various directions, accompanied by snarls and grunts, Mr Wortnall finally lost his temper and wrenched the joystick out of its panel in a shower of sparks. He was left dangling at a ridiculous angle, looking stupid, with the joystick in his hand, wires hanging out like roots.

'Drive!' Mr Wortnall shouted, and the car jerked ahead, braking suddenly, causing the crane to shoot forward, bumping Mr Wortnall's head against the wall.

'You idiot!' he screamed at the driver.

'Sorry, sir,' a muffled voice said inside the car.

Finally level with the black square in the wall, Mr Wortnall reached up and pressed it with his thumb. The square turned green and emitted a digital pinging sound. A computerised voice came from somewhere inside the wall: '*Fingerprint identified. Mr C. G. Wortnall. Entry permitted.*'

As Freddy and Minnie watched, part of the wall moved outwards and swung up, revealing an entrance. The shark-car shot inside the factory, passing two enormous guards in uniform, who looked like human bulldogs. There didn't seem to be any join between their immense meaty necks and their immense meaty heads. One of them was about

to pull a lever to close the door when the other shouted: 'Wait!' and pointed up to the sky.

A swarm of crows was circling directly over where Freddy and Minnie were hiding, weaving in and out of the smog.

'The crowbots are excited today, Mr Troff,' the first guard said. He had an immense meaty voice, to match the rest of him.

'You're right, Mr Peek,' said the other one.

'It's almost as if they've spotted two children hiding in the grass, possibly a boy with blondish hair and a girl with glasses eating biscuits or something.'

'He's good at guessing,' Minnie said, in a hushed voice.

Freddy tutted. 'Don't be stupid! They're watching us, using those crow-things! They must have cameras built into them!'

The furious beating of wings grew louder as the swarm of crowbots spiralled towards them in a kind of whirlpool. A bank of flickering TV monitors inside the factory door showed Minnie and Freddy from a variety of angles.

'What are we going to do?' Minnie cried, jumping up.

Looking round for a solution, Freddy had a sudden burst of inspiration.

'Quick! Stand on my *You-Shoes*!'

'What?'

'GET ON!'

Minnie hopped onto Freddy's feet and faced him as if they were ballroom dancers, trying to keep her balance as he clicked the dial on his *Gavins* up to DASH!

'Hold on tight!' he said.

The shoes sprang up, heading for the path, gaining momentum.

THUMP, THUMP, THUMP, THUMP, THUMP!

Behind them they heard the bulldog-men laughing as they watched the children disappear into the fog.

'Send the birds after them,' said Mr Troff.

'Yes, Mr Troff,' said Mr Peek, and flicked a switch under the monitors.

All the way down the hill, as Freddy's *You-Shoes* sped on and Minnie tried not to slide off, the crowbots ducked and dived, sometimes skimming Freddy's and Minnie's heads so closely that the tips of their metal claws and beaks snagged their hair. The air was full of electronic shrieks and cries.

'*ARRRRK! ARRRRK! ARRRRK!*'

Running past the signs on their way down, they saw on the back of them were written things like: 'GOOD RIDDANCE! YOU'RE FINALLY GOING!' and 'GREAT! DON'T COME BACK!'

As soon as they were out of the brown mist, the crowbots gave up and drifted back to the top of the hill, their work done.

Freddy's *Gavins* were extremely hot, and even after

the two children had collapsed in an exhausted heap on a hedge by the smelly farm, they kept twitching.

*

The children walked home through the town hardly saying a word to each other. The attempt to see Mr Wortnall had been a complete failure and they were both rather shaken by it.

Minnie's father suddenly appeared in front of them, red-faced with anger. He had been to the school to find out why his daughter hadn't come home and was furious to learn she had been seen leaving with Bert Bird's son. Mr Carstairs grabbed her by the wrist and marched her off.

As Freddy headed up the path to his house, he heard Minnie's front door slam shut, followed by the sound of shouting. He could just make out her father saying: 'What were you doing with that boy? After all his father's done to us!' Freddy wished he could go round to the Carstairses and explain how they'd been trying to make things better. But he knew, being grown-ups, they wouldn't understand.

Catching sight of himself in his bedroom mirror, Freddy noticed his *Gavins* were no longer their original midnight blue but were now a nasty brown from the factory's dust. He thumped the mirror, angrily. There was no way a skinny boy with dirty shoes was ever going to stand up to an enemy as powerful as Mr C. G. Wortnall.

6

THE GARDEN MYSTERY

Over the next few weeks Freddy tried get on with life as usual. But things were different now.

For instance, every morning Mrs Carstairs marched Minnie to school herself, clutching her hand tightly like a prison warden. Whenever they passed Freddy, she sped up and the most Minnie could do was exchange some sort of grimace with him over her shoulder.

Freddy caught glimpses of Minnie's unemployed father sitting sadly in the front room of his house, surrounded by shoeboxes. Sometimes he would lift out a boot or a sandal, then quickly put it away again, overcome with emotion. Footwear was his life. Nothing came between him and his shoes (except his socks, of course).

At the same time Freddy began to notice his own dad acting strangely.

One night Freddy woke up from a bad dream in which he was being chased across a bleak open desert by a massive crowbot with Mr Wortnall riding on its back. When he padded across to his dad's room to tell him about his nightmare, he found the bed hadn't been slept in. Tiptoeing downstairs still half asleep, he caught Bert sneaking into the back garden, carrying a large grey sack with something inside it that clunked. His dad looked startled to see him.

'What are you doing, Dad?' Freddy asked.

'Oh, just thought I'd tidy up the – um – garden a bit,' he said.

'But it's the middle of the night.'

'Is it? Oh, *that's* why it's dark.'

'What's in that sack?'

'Just some garden tools,' said Bert.

It was obvious he was lying because 1) his dad never tidied anything, and 2) the only time he went in the garden was to look for something in the shed (which was piled up with junk, like the rest of the house). This was why the back garden was a wilderness of weeds with a forgotten pond somewhere in the middle of it.

It was all very odd.

*

Freddy and Minnie began to lead secretive lives, observing their parents' behaviour and reporting to one another via the *Ear to Ear* communicators. This was now the only way they could talk when they were not at school. But they had to be careful not to let anyone find out.

For this reason Minnie usually spoke to Freddy from the bathroom, so there was often the gush of running water or a flushing sound. Their conversations usually started with Minnie's voice hissing through the ear at him: 'Is that – *gurgle* – you – *splash* – Freddy?'

And he would have to ask her to angle her 'ear' away from the taps.

If Minnie's mum and dad hadn't been so distracted by their own worries, they might have wondered why she'd started taking fifteen baths a day.

*

One Saturday afternoon they were chatting through the *Ear to Ear*s when Minnie suddenly shouted: 'FREDDY!' very loudly.

'OW! Can you not shout so loudly in your ear?' he said.

'Your dad's in the garden again. Down at the end in all the brambles.'

Freddy had asked Minnie to alert him whenever she saw Bert outside, so he could find out what his dad was up to.

He ran out of his bedroom and skidded across the bathroom floor in his socks, clutching his *Ear to Ear* device.

He looked down from the window into the garden but it was empty.

'He's not there now,' he whispered into the ear.

'He must be. He was by that statue thing a second ago,' Minnie insisted. 'I saw him!'

Freddy hurried out, pushing his way through the brambles to a concrete statue of a cherub holding a bow and arrow – which was supposed to be Cupid, the God of Love, but to Freddy just looked like a fat, grumpy baby.

'Dad?' he called, walking round the statue. 'Dad? Where are you?'

There was no one there.

He wondered if Bert could have slipped through a gap

in the fence into another garden, but after an extensive search he couldn't see a way out. He looked up at Minnie, framed in her bedroom window.

'He's definitely not here,' he whispered into the ear device.

'He can't have just disappeared,' she said, puzzled. 'Check again.'

Freddy walked round the garden three more times but there was no sign of his father so he went indoors.

He had only been inside a moment when the back door burst open and his dad walked in.

Freddy's jaw dropped open.

'All right, Fred?' his dad said, as if nothing was out of the ordinary.

'But – where have you been?' Freddy stammered.

'Down by the pond, clearing brambles,' Bert said.

His dad was lying.

What was going on?

*

Later that night there was a knock on Freddy's bedroom door. 'Do you want to play Fat Nan the Boxer?' his dad asked, peering in and holding up a deck of cards.

Fat Nan the Boxer was a card game Freddy had played with his dad ever since he could remember. It was quite complicated with lots of silly rules they had made up, including hiding cards and running around the room with cushions up your jumper.

'I've got some biscuits,' his dad said. 'And some custard to dip them in.'

After the disturbing things that had been happening, it was a relief to spend some time together, having fun. Whenever they played cards, Bert seemed not to notice the time, so Freddy got to stay up late and listen to cool music. His dad had wired the house up with its own sound system, using old horn speakers from garden fetes, which he hung in the corners of each room. When they were turned up full, the whole house shook with music and the water in the fish tank trembled so much that Elvis the goldfish appeared to be wiggling his hips.

The longer they played Fat Nan, the faster and more hilarious it got until eventually Bert yawned widely and looked at his watch: 'Is that the time, Fred? I'd better get to bed. Big day tomorrow.'

'Why? What's happening?' Freddy asked.

'Oh. Nothing! Just things to do,' Bert said quickly, tucking him in.

But although he smiled, Freddy could tell he was

hiding something. Bert clicked out the light, then hung round in the doorway staring back at Freddy.

'What is it, Dad?'

'Er, love you,' he said.

'Yeah, love you, Dad.'

It was late and Freddy's eyes felt heavy. It wasn't long before he was back running through the desert with Wortnall on the crowbot flying after him. He was so sound asleep that he didn't hear Minnie's voice buzzing at him from the *Ear to Ear* under his pillow: 'Freddy? Are you there? Wake up!'

*

In her room next door, Minnie had also been up late – trying to finish building a volcano out of chicken wire and newspaper for a school project – when she had noticed a light flashing in Freddy's garden.

Looking out, she watched with fascination as Bert Bird made his way through the tall weeds again, swinging a torch. He had another sack over his shoulder, bulging with shapes. As he disappeared behind a mound of brambles, she saw the torchlight bobbing round and his dark outline by the Cupid statue.

Then, suddenly, he was gone.

Vanished.

Into thin air.

7

MINNIE'S VOLCANO

'What do you mean "vanished into thin air"?' Freddy said.

'Well, I *think* it was thin. You can't get *thick* air, can you?' She held out a bag of sweets. 'Lemon-jellycat?'

'No thanks. Just tell me what happened.'

It was lunchtime at school next day and the first chance Minnie had had to tell Freddy about his disappearing father.

'It was the same as last time,' she said. 'One minute he was there in the garden, large as life. Then he wasn't.'

'Look, I don't care if my dad's signed a secret contract thing with Wortnall, I want to know what's going on. I'm going to make him tell me everything tonight.'

The bell rang out. The children lined up in the playground in their different classes before going in to lessons. Mr Brimpton, the rather sweaty, nervous Geography teacher, cleared his throat and clapped for attention:

'Er, children? – I have a small – er – er—'

'Brain?' somebody shouted.

Everyone laughed.

'WHO SAID THAT?' Mr Brimpton stared along the lines of children.

Mr Keeping, the Music teacher, raised his hand. '*I* did.' He leant closer to Mr Brimpton: 'Just my little joke, Graham.'

'Yes, well, highly amusing,' Mr Brimpton snorted. 'Anyway, er, er – er – children, I have a small er – er – ANNOUNCEMENT,' he stared hard at Mr Keeping to stop him interrupting. 'Now, the Year 4s have been – er – er – set a task to construct the – er – er – model of an active – er – er – er – volcano.'

'Get on with it!' came a shout.

'RIGHT, WHO SAID THAT?'

The Headteacher raised his hand. '*I* did. And I'm *not* joking, Brimpton. Hurry up.'

'Oh. Sorry, sir,' Mr Brimpton muttered, nervously. 'So I would – er – like to announce that the winning pupil of the – er – Best Volcano is – er – er – er – Minnie Carstairs!'

'Well done, Minnie!' said Freddy.

Everyone clapped as she was called forward to hold up her model. It was rather good. For a finishing touch, she had dripped wax from some posh red candles down the sides, to look like lava.

She held the model high above her head in triumph.

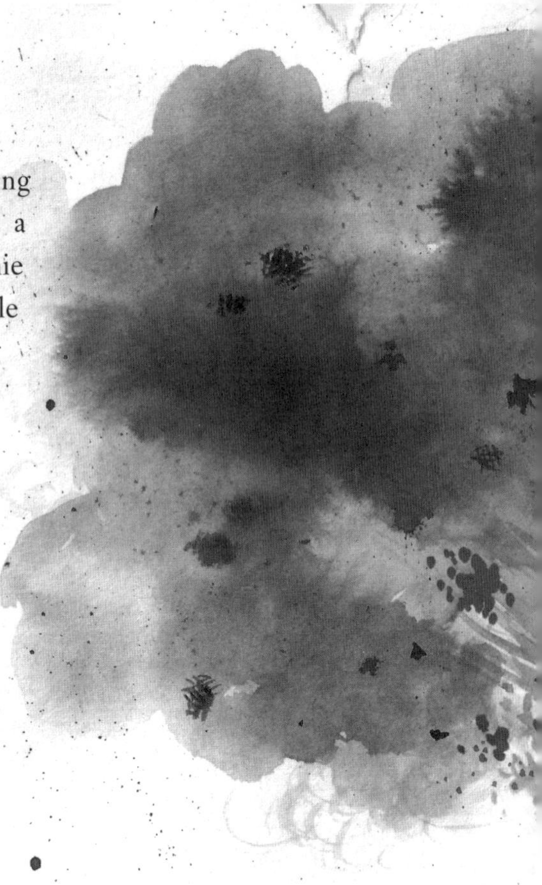

The clapping had just reached a climax and Minnie was trying to smile without showing the Lemon-jellycat wedged in her cheek, when there was a bang as loud as thunder and a huge explosion seemed to blast out of the middle of the volcano into the sky.

After a shocked pause, the whole school cheered and applauded.

'Er – er – how did she do *that*?' gasped Mr Brimpton.

'Fireworks?' Mr Keeping suggested.

But as Minnie lowered the model, they could see the explosion had in fact come from the factory on the hill behind.

'Look!' said the Head, pointing to a plume of black

smoke billowing up through the fog on the summit of the hill, like ink separating through milk.

'Quickly. Get everyone inside,' he ordered the teachers.

As Miss Arbourteel shepherded excited pupils into the school building, telling them to stay calm, Freddy stood rooted to the spot, looking up at the factory. He could see flickers of gold flame like hungry tongues reaching over the outside wall.

'Dad…' he said, under his breath. He felt numb.

It was only when everyone was back in class that Miss Arbourteel noticed Freddy's empty desk.

'Where is Freddy Bird?' she snapped.

Minnie pointed outside.

Freddy was still in the playground, staring up at the hill in disbelief. Smoke from the explosion was starting to drift across the town. The sound of shrieking sirens echoed off buildings as emergency vehicles hurried towards the factory.

Miss Arbourteel poked her head out of the main doors of the school, gesturing urgently: 'Freddy! Inside!'

Glancing back, Freddy saw his classmates' faces pressed against the windows, watching.

'FREDERIC!' Miss Arbourteel barked. 'COME INSIDE! NOW!'

Freddy started to walk in the opposite direction, across the playground and out of the school gates. It felt like a nightmare where everything was in slow motion or as if he were walking underwater. He didn't hear Miss Arbourteel calling. He just kept walking through the streets towards the hill.

People were leaning out of their windows or had stopped their cars and were staring up at the cloud of darkness spreading across the town. He passed the house with the yappy dog, then the farm with the nosy cow, a burning smell growing stronger with every step. Several fire engines were parked at the bottom of the hill. Freddy continued past a group of firemen talking urgently.

'It's too steep! We'll never get the engines up!'

They didn't notice Freddy slipping past them till

he was halfway up the hill, when one of the firefighters shouted after him: 'Hey! Where are you going? Come back! It's dangerous!'

But all Freddy could think about was his dad. He had to find him and make sure he was all right.

As he climbed higher and higher towards the factory, he began to walk faster, his eyes fixed on the walls in the distance. He had forgotten he was wearing his *Gavins* and could have set them to DASH!

The sound of crackling flames grew steadily louder, mixed with the distressed croak of crowbots, circling above the fire in wild formations, their feathers lit up from beneath, all red and orange.

Reaching the factory at last, Freddy could hear alarms blaring inside. He hammered on the wall with his fists. 'LET ME IN!' The alarms were deafening and his voice seemed very small. He tried to leap up and touch the small black square, which Mr Wortnall had pressed to operate the door. But he was too short to reach it. He looked round for something to stand on. There was nothing except cracked earth and gravel.

Gravel! That might do!

He began to pile handfuls into a mound against the wall. After a few minutes' frantic scooping his hands were covered in scratches but the mound was high enough to stand on. He climbed carefully onto it. The gravel shifted under his feet, pattering away in little trickles but, steadying himself, he reached up as far as he could stretch. He was still centimetres from the square.

'Come on. You can do it,' he said, willing himself on.

Standing on tiptoe, he stretched out his palm and then his fingers. At full stretch, his thumb just reached the square.

He pressed it.

Instead of turning green, however, as it had for Mr Wortnall, the black square went red and an automated voice barked: '*Fingerprint not recognised. Entry denied.*'

The wall stayed resolutely shut. Freddy slumped against it, not sure what to do. As he did so, he heard something mechanical moving on the other side.

Suddenly he was being lifted off the ground! The wall was swinging open from inside, with him on it!

In seconds, he was high up in the air, lying on a metal shelf, like an open garage door. Peering over the edge, he saw smoke puff out of the entrance below. Then, with a growl, Mr Wortnall's shark-car sped out and disappeared down the hill.

Freddy could see into the factory for the first time. Ahead lay a tunnel, snaking off into the building. Echoing somewhere far down it he heard shouts and the shrill wail of fire alarms. Freddy crawled carefully to the edge of the metal roof. It was quite a drop but it didn't even cross his mind that he might hurt himself. He just wanted to get inside and find his dad.

He hit the ground with a thump and scrambled to his feet.

The monitors inside the door, transmitting what the crowbots saw, displayed images of the fire from many different angles, a churning inferno billowing smoke. The birds were swooping overhead in an agitated state, so all the screens looked wobbly. Freddy turned and started to run down the tunnel. Almost at once the two guards, Troff and Peek, appeared, stomping towards him.

'It's that boy again, Mr Troff!'

'I can see that, Mr Peek.' Troff turned and called to Freddy, 'Oi, you! Stop!'

This time he didn't try to escape. The men strode up to him. They were smeared with soot, having just come from the fire.

'No one's allowed in here! You're trespassing!' Troff grunted.

'Grab him, Peek.'

'Yes, Mr Troff.'

They picked Freddy up on either side and marched him back to the entrance, legs dangling in the air between them.

'Get off me. I've got to find my dad. He works here – his name's Bert Bird.'

'*Him!* Mr Wortnall's very angry with him,' Troff grunted.

'He's in a lot of trouble!' said Peek.

'Where is he? I want to see him!' said Freddy, trying to wriggle free.

'Go on, clear off,' said Mr Troff, shoving Freddy out onto the hill.

Mr Peek pulled the lever, which closed the factory entrance. It started to rattle shut.

'Wait! I've *got* to find my dad!' Freddy yelled at them. His whole body had gone cold and there was a sudden choking feeling in his throat, like he'd swallowed an apple – whole.

'Go away!' Mr Troff shouted.

Then the wall clanged shut, leaving him alone on the hillside.

8

CUPID'S BOTTOM

Freddy sat in his kitchen in silence. It was getting dark but it hadn't crossed his mind to put the lights on. He felt stunned, as if someone had whacked him hard on the head.

He looked at the clock: 6.32 p.m. He could hear the second-hand ticking loudly. Then he noticed the sound of the tap dripping as well.

Tick

Drip

Tick

Drip

Tick

Drip.

6.33. His dad still wasn't home. Freddy had walked back through town from the factory in a daze and had been slumped at the kitchen table ever since.

When his head jerked suddenly upwards, he realised he must have dozed off. The clock now said nothing because it was pitch black and he couldn't see it. He got up and turned on the light.

8.17 p.m.

Bert was *always* back by seven.

Freddy kept telling himself everything would be okay. In a few minutes, life would be back to normal and his dad would come bursting through the door and cook him Brussels sprouts with chocolate sauce or something.

He got up. There was a miaow above. Timmy was hungry. As Freddy paced through the dark house, the cat buzzed after him at shoulder height. He was settling into his new existence as an airborne cat and had learnt to propel himself round the rooms by pushing his little back legs off the walls. (It was handy to be that high up for chasing moths.)

A thought struck Freddy. Perhaps his dad had come in while he was sleeping! It would be just like Bert not to disturb him. But all the rooms were horribly silent and full of things that reminded him of his dad: the mess of machinery, calculations on the walls, odd-coloured shoes and the ladies' fur coat hanging in the hall.

In the front room he came across one of his dad's unfinished inventions, the *Voice-Translation System.* Bert hadn't got far with it, having only recorded the English phrases to be translated into other languages. Freddy clunked it on. The slowed-down recording lurched up to normal speed and his father's voice blared from the speaker: *'I would like to buy a suitcase, please… Is this lobster fresh?… I would prefer this in purple…'*

Just hearing his dad made Freddy even sadder. He sank down on a chair, choking back tears. Then, *SCRRRAPE!*

He heard the front gate opening and footsteps approaching.

'Dad!'

Freddy hurtled into the hallway, beaming with joy. He pulled the front door open. His heart sank. It was Miss Arbourteel.

'Ah, *bonsoir*, Frederic, I came to check you were all right,' she said. 'You should not have run away from school like that.'

'I'm sorry, Miss,' said Freddy, trying to hide his disappointment.

'Is your father home safely from the factory?'

Freddy's mind worked fast. He didn't want to leave the house in case his dad came back and he was sure Miss Arbourteel wouldn't let him stay there alone.

'Yes,' he lied, trying to sound casual. 'He's fine. He's on the phone at the moment.'

As they listened, they could hear Bert's voice from the machine in the front room, saying: *'Please help me. I need to find the nearest police station.'*

Puzzled by this, Miss Arbourteel tried to peer past Freddy into the house. She caught sight of writing up the wall and the floor strewn with junk. Then she noticed what looked like a cat flying past.

'Is everything all right, Frederic?' she said, trying to force her way inside.

'Yes. Perfectly. Thank you. Goodnight.'

Freddy slammed the door on her.

Outside, Miss Arbourteel paused as she walked past the lounge window. Inside she could hear Bert saying slowly and clearly: *'I would like to buy a single ticket to Morocco for tomorrow morning.'*

My god, she thought, he's abandoning his son!

As she made her way home, she decided something must be done.

*

After Miss Arbourteel had gone, Freddy lay down on his bed in his clothes. The *Ear to Ear* device buzzed by his bedside.

'Freddy? – *gurgle* – Are you there? – *splash*,' said Minnie.

'Yes, I'm here,' he said, in a wobbly voice. He had been trying not to burst into tears for several hours.

'You sound terrible. Are you all right?'

'No. My dad's not home yet. I don't know what's happened to him.' A hot tear trickled down his face. He wiped it away on his sleeve.

'Wait! My mum's coming!' said Minnie. There was the

sound of a toilet flushing and the ear went dead.

Freddy lay back and let the tears flow out of him until he imagined his face looked like Minnie's volcano, all red and dribbly. But after a few minutes an intense feeling came over him that he shouldn't be crying. After all there were still important mysteries to be solved. For instance, his dad's strange behaviour in the back garden. That seemed a good place to start.

He pulled on his father's wellies (which were five sizes too big) at the back door and, clicking on his torch, made his way outside. Trampling down brambles and nettles, he reached the stone cherub in the wilderness, where Minnie had seen his dad disappear. He got down on all fours to search for clues, swinging his torch beam over the weedy ground. His knees were soon covered in scratches and all he found was a grill from an old barbecue and the partly chewed head of a doll Minnie had thrown over the fence during a tantrum many years before.

He was about to give up and go back indoors when the moon came out from behind a cloud and shone down, lighting up the statue. Freddy did a double take.

It was facing the wrong way!

Cupid's bow and arrow was normally aimed at the house, but for some reason its horrible fat bottom was now pointing there instead. Freddy pushed against the statue. With a scraping sound, it moved.

There was something below it! It was covering a hole!

Putting his shoulder to it, he pushed the statue with all his strength. Gradually, it moved aside, revealing the entrance to a large, rusty pipe with the words 'Property of the Water Board' etched around the rim. He shone his torch down it and saw the rungs of a ladder leading into darkness. So *this* was where his dad had been going!

He swung himself into the hole and started to climb down, clenching the torch between his teeth so he could keep his hands free.

After a few rungs however, his foot slipped in the oversized wellies and he cried out. The torch plummeted into darkness, thudding to the ground with a resounding echo a few seconds later.

'Please don't let it be broken,' he said to himself.

Gulping, he looked down and could just make out a pool of light far below at the bottom of the shaft.

He continued his descent, gripping the ladder tighter than ever. The pipe smelt musty and the walls were dripping wet. Glancing up, he could see the moonlit sky as a small silvery circle a long way up. At the bottom of the ladder, he picked up his torch, which was still shining, and swung it round, taking in his surroundings. He was in an old water pipe, the height of a room. Dotted across the floor were old grey sacks like the one he'd seen his dad sneaking into the garden with. Pulling one open, he jumped back in shock as a metal foot, shaped like a human's, flopped out.

His cry echoed round the tunnel.

Lifting the foot out carefully, he found it was connected to a metal leg. The steel bones had coloured wires twisted around them; coils of pink and red like muscles, with a network of veiny blue ones on top. He was staring at it in wonder, when there was a whir and the leg suddenly drew back at the knee joint and gave him a hard kick. Freddy fell back on the floor, winded.

The leg jumped up and began hopping round.

'Stop!' Freddy said. 'Come back!'

Ignoring him, the leg leapt off down the tunnel. He

ran after it, trying to grab it in his outstretched hands. But it was too fast. The leg bounced off the wall and jumped back at him, so he had to duck to avoid getting kicked in the teeth. Finally, after a frantic chase, Freddy threw himself onto it and wrestled it to the ground where the leg thrashed under him like a fish out of water. After a few seconds it went quiet as if its power had run out. Only the big toe twitched.

As Freddy lay there getting his breath back, he noticed a large well-thumbed notebook with a battered red cover lying in the shadows. The word 'DROID' was written on

the front in big letters. Under it, stamped in green ink, was Mr C. G. Wortnall's logo.

He opened the book and began leafing through it. There was page after page of drawings and calculations; detailed sketches of robotic hands and complicated circuits. One showed the idea for an electronic brain, labelled with things like 'memory circuits', 'speech box', 'movement controller'. Another showed a small motor with wires snaking out of it, shaped like a heart.

Flicking back to the first page, Freddy read a coffee-stained entry scrawled by his father: '*Mr Wortnall has asked me to begin a new project; to create a droid that will look and act exactly like a human being. This is the most challenging project of my life and the most exciting. I'm not sure if it's even possible. But I'm going to try.*'

His dad had been building this for Mr Wortnall, so why had he brought it back from the factory and hidden it here?

Freddy got up and looked in the other sacks. They contained other parts of a droid: an electronic arm, a metal ribcage, a spine. The torch began to flicker. The batteries were running out. The last thing Freddy wanted was to be stuck underground in a scary tunnel in pitch darkness with robotic limbs chasing after him.

Making his way back to the ladder, he noticed a peg on the wall with a smaller sack hanging off it, weighed down by what looked like a football. Lifting it down cautiously, he peered inside and could just make out some sort of mechanical head. As he turned it round to look at the face, he gasped in shock.

It was a replica of a face he knew well.

His dad was staring back at him!

Then, with a fizz, the torch went out.

9

THE DRIBBS

'Well?' asked Minnie, as they traipsed down the corridor to their first lesson the next day. 'Did your dad come back?'

Freddy was suddenly alert. 'Sssh!' he said, 'I don't want anybody knowing.'

'Knowing what?'

He pulled her aside. 'No, he didn't come home. The guards at the factory told me he's in big trouble.'

'But the explosion, Freddy! Is he all right?'

'I don't know yet. I don't know what's going on.'

He was about to tell Minnie all about the 'droid' when a familiar voice came ringing out:

'*Frederic! Un moment, please!*'

Freddy swung round. Miss Arbourteel was at the end of the corridor with a serious-looking man and woman in suits, clutching briefcases. They both had grey hair, pointy glasses and pale skinny faces that looked like someone had squashed them in a door. Miss Arbourteel gestured Freddy over:

'Frederic, this is Mr and Miss Dribb. They would like to talk to you.'

The Dribbs bent forward, holding out business cards in their limp grey hands; they made all their movements at exactly the same time. Freddy realised they must be twins.

'We are from a department called the "Protection of Orphans, Families and Children, Etcetera",' said the lady. She had a whiny voice like a fly. She was trying to smile but her mouth didn't look like it was capable of it.

Freddy took the card and looked at it. It said:

'It says "Poo-face",' he said.

'Yes, we know!' the man snapped angrily. 'It's too late to change it now. We've had all the stationery printed!'

'People are always pointing that out,' Miss Dribb spat. 'It's very irritating!'

'Anyway, that's beside the point. If we are not satisfied you're being cared for properly, young man, we can take you away,' said Mr Dribb coldly.

'For your own *protection*,' Miss Dribb added. But it didn't sound convincing.

They whipped out clipboards with nasty printed forms on them.

'Parent or guardian's name?'

'Um, Bert Bird.'

'"Umbert", is that *one* "M" or *two*?'

'No. It's just Bert. With a "B".'

'You said *"Umbert"*! Make up your mind! – Age?'

'Eleven and a half.'

'Your *father*'s eleven and a half? Don't try to be funny!'

'Oh, my *dad*'s age.'

'Yes, boy! Pay attention!'

'I'm not sure. About forty-five?'

'Your teacher tells us your house is full of junk. Has your parent or guardian ever dropped a heavy object *onto* or *near to* you?'

'Er… yes. Once. Years ago.'

The Dribbs gasped and started writing frantically on their forms.

'It didn't hurt me though!' Freddy gabbled. He didn't like the Dribbs or their trick questions. 'Our house is always full of machines and things.'

'WHAT?' Miss Dribb cried.

'Right,' said Mr Dribb. 'Put down "dangerous machinery"!'

They started scribbling even faster, eyes full of excitement.

Freddy tried to stop them. 'Wait! It's not dangerous,' he said. 'My dad's an inventor! They're things he's working on!'

Mr Dribb pointed down at Freddy's school bag with his pen. 'Show me your lunch box.'

Freddy brought it out. The Dribbs peered in as he peeled back the lid. Mr Dribb lifted out a mouldy banana skin.

'Is this how your parent-stroke-guardian feeds you?'

'I shall write down, "diet inappropriate",' said Miss Dribb eagerly.

'Yes!' said Mr Dribb.

They were enjoying themselves now.

'Very well! We shall be coming round to your house to pay you a surprise visit,' said Miss Dribb, with relish.

'W-when?' Freddy stammered.

'We're not telling you *that*! It wouldn't be a surprise!'

The Dribbs slid their clipboards into their briefcases and clicked them shut.

'Tell your father the department for the Protection of Orphans, Families and Children, Etcetera will be coming to assess you.'

'Or "Poo-face",' said Freddy.

'No, not *Poo-face*,' said Mr Dribb. 'It's not *Poo-face*, I don't want to hear anybody call it *Poo-face* ever again, all right?'

They strode off down the corridor, glancing back at him darkly.

Miss Arbourteel seemed a little shocked.

'I'm sorry, Freddy. I brought them here because I was worried about you last night. I was only trying to help,' she said, rather flustered.

'Everything's fine, Miss. Honestly,' Freddy lied, blushing bright red.

'Don't worry,' Minnie said as they hurried to their lesson. 'Your dad might be back when you get home tonight.'

*

But he wasn't. The house was cold and dark when Freddy got in.

He hadn't been back long when the letter box clacked open, making him jump. He was on edge, expecting the Dribbs on their surprise visit.

'It's me!' Minnie's freckly face peered in. 'My parents have gone out. You said you had something to show me.'

'Yes! Come on!'

Freddy dragged her into the back garden.

'Where are we going?'

'You'll see.'

At the bottom of the garden, among the weeds and brambles, he heaved the statue of the cherub aside and pointed down into the dark hole.

Too amazed to say anything, Minnie followed him down the ladder. This time Freddy brought a camping light, which lit the dripping walls with a warm glow. Once they were at the bottom, he took the droid's head from the sack where it was hanging. Minnie recoiled in disgust, seeing what looked like Bert Bird's head in his hands. Freddy tossed it to her:

'It's okay. It's not an *actual* head.'

Turning it over, Minnie could see wires and circuits hanging out of the back.

'It's some sort of robot,' she said, in wonder.

'A droid,' said Freddy.

'What's the skin made of?' Minnie prodded the fleshy substance.

'Some sort of rubber jelly,' said Freddy. 'Looks like my dad moulded it from his own face.'

As she moved the head, the droid's eyes wobbled up and down like a doll's.

'Aagh!' yelped Minnie, nearly dropping it. 'It looked at me!'

One by one they emptied all the sacks and soon the separate parts of the metallic man lay in a heap around them.

‘This is incredible!’ Minnie gasped. ‘Your dad really is a genius.’

‘Watch that leg. It’s got a mind of its own.’ Freddy pointed to the robotic limb that had given him so much trouble the night before.

‘And there’s a kind of log my dad was keeping.’ Freddy handed her his father’s notebook.

She leafed through it with growing excitement. ‘It’s like the stuff we’ve been doing in computer club, only a thousand times more advanced.’

‘I’ve worked out how I can fool those horrible Dribb people!’ Freddy said. ‘But I’ll need your help.’

Minnie looked up, expectantly.

Freddy fixed her with a determined stare. ‘We’re going to build Dad Droid!’

10

GONNA GET DIS GROOVY TING TOGEVVA

'We're back, Minnie,' Mrs Carstairs called out, coming through the front door. Minnie looked up from her homework, trying to slow her breathing because only seconds earlier she had scrambled over the fence from next door and run through the house, plonking herself down at the table just in time. She was still rather flushed.

'Are you all right, darling? You look very red,' her mum said.

'Yes, I'm fine,' said Minnie.

'Have you got a temperature?' Her mum felt Minnie's forehead with the back of her hand. 'You *do* feel rather hot.'

'Actually, now you mention it I am feeling a bit funny,' Minnie said, jumping at the chance to excuse herself. 'I'm going to bed.'

Her mother looked surprised. 'Oh, all right. Goodnight then, darling.'

'Goodnight.'

Heading upstairs, Minnie saw her father entering the house, looking miserable. Every day he seemed a bit smaller and more worn down by his worries. She smiled at him and he smiled tightly back.

She hurried upstairs, passing shoeboxes on every step. Mr Carstairs couldn't bear to get rid of his beloved shoes, so there were boxes everywhere: under the beds, filling the drawers. Whenever you opened a cupboard, a whole wall of them would fall on top of you. Now of course they were worthless because the whole town only wanted *You-Shoes.*

Minnie had to wait for hours for her parents to go to bed before she could sneak back to Freddy's house. Finally, when the top stair creaked a second time, she knew they must both be in their room and it was safe to go. She arranged pillows under the covers to make it look like she was lying there, in case her mum looked in. She even stuck a wig on top, that she'd found in a box at Freddy's, which matched her hair exactly.

It was a good job she did, because half an hour after Minnie had crept out, her mum came into the room and sat down on her daughter's bed in the darkness, launching into a heartfelt speech about change and moving on and how brave she knew Minnie was going to be. When she got up to go, she stroked Minnie's hair, thinking how clean it was, and left, feeling closer than she had ever felt to her daughter, unaware she had in fact been talking to a couple of old pillows and a hairpiece.

*

'Right,' said Minnie, coming through the back door of Freddy's house. 'Let's start.'

While she'd been gone, Freddy had brought all the parts of the droid inside and laid them out on the dining-room table, where they looked rather gruesome, especially the very real-looking head with Bert's face on it, which was now perched on a vase.

Clicking on the light above the table, the dining room transformed into a makeshift operating theatre. There was even a trolley with his dad's tools on it, which Freddy had gone through the house collecting. (This was actually a sweet trolley for displaying puddings, but it fitted its new purpose perfectly.) On the shelves below the tools were boxes of nuts and bolts and several clumps of coloured wire from one of the sacks.

Freddy gave Minnie a white lab coat belonging to his dad, pulling on another himself. They were far too big for them so they had to roll up the sleeves and try not to trip over the tails, but once they were wearing them, they looked like proper scientists.

He handed her his dad's notebook. 'You read out the instructions, I'll build it.' He was eager to get going and picked up a screwdriver as if he knew what he was doing.

But Minnie soon discovered there weren't exactly any 'instructions' in Bert's book. It was more a series of splurges direct from his incredible brain.

After a lot of page-turning and some heavy sighs, she decided the best way to start was by putting the basic skeleton together. It took both of them pushing and pulling and twisting and clicking to get the first leg attached to the hip socket. It wasn't till they had connected the second one that Minnie realised the hips were in fact shoulders and they had to start all over again.

When they did eventually get the legs in the right place, they had to feed hundreds of complicated wires through the bone structure, which was a fiddly business and soon led to arguments.

'You said the *blue* wire!'

'No, I didn't! I said *red*!'

'Give *me* the screwdriver!'

'No, *I'll* do it!'

'*I* will!'

'*I* will!'

To help them stay awake, Freddy put one of his dad's favourite songs, 'Gonna Get Dis Groovy Ting Togevva' by the Dendy-Krepp Trio, on the home-made sound system. The funky music, blasting through the horns in the corners of the room, made them work much faster:

Gonna get dis groovy ting togevva
In my mamma's best home-knitted sweatta
Wid da moosic twangin' round an' round
Like a groovy gravy made of sound…

*

Three hours later a fully formed droid was lying on the table, minus its head. Hundreds of wires were sticking out of the neck, all of which had to be connected to circuit boards in the brain.

This was where Minnie's computer classes came in handy as she had already built several basic robots, including an insect that could find its way round mazes and a metal cube with wheels that didn't really do anything except spin in circles and fall off desks. Using the magnifying glass from Freddy's bug-collecting kit, Minnie concentrated on connecting the delicate wires, consulting Bert's diagrams. Her eyes were heavy from lack of sleep and it felt as if someone had rubbed salt under her lids – but at last she was fixing the final wire into place, which was 'Orange 777A, Nerve ending to the left eyebrow'.

Together she and Freddy fitted the droid's head onto its neck and stood back to admire their creation. It had been a long night. They were both more tired than they had ever been before but they were bubbling with excitement.

'Stay there a minute,' Freddy said, and ran out of the room. He came back a moment later with a bundle of his father's clothes. After a few minutes of lifting stiff limbs and forcing hands through sleeves, the droid was dressed exactly like Bert Bird. As a finishing touch Freddy gave him a pair of mismatched shoes from the hallway: one yellow and one brown, just like his dad would wear. Then they hauled the droid off the table and into the chair by the window, which was Bert's favourite place to sit. In the pinky-gold light of dawn, filtering through the net curtains, it could have been his dad sitting there.

'We've done it, Minnie! It's complete!'

Freddy stepped forward and gave the droid a gentle prod, expecting it to come to life. But its head just lolled to one side.

'It's not working,' he groaned. 'How do we switch it on?'

Suddenly, everything they'd done seemed pointless and they were as far from bringing the droid to life as when they'd started. Minnie flicked through the book to a section called 'Power supply connection', which looked even longer and more complex than the previous entries. 'I'll have to read this through and work it out.'

She glanced at the clock, giving a wide yawn.

'It's nearly five in the morning. I'd better get back before my mum wakes up.' She tucked the battered notebook under her arm and headed out. 'See you later, Freddy. And well done.'

'Thanks, Minnie.'

After the back door closed behind her, Freddy went over to the chair where the droid was slumped and sat at its feet, the way he used to with his dad. Tiredness came rushing over him and before he knew it, he had fallen back against the droid's legs in a deep sleep.

Rays from the rising sun speared in through a gap in the curtains and spread across the carpet, growing wider and more golden. The swelling violins of Uncle Oony's Orchestra – another of Bert's favourite bands – began to play through the horns in the corners. As Freddy turned in

his sleep, the robot fell forward in the chair and one of its arms swung across him, as if it were protecting him.

11

CAT POWER

Minnie was woken by the sound of hammering outside her window.

After getting home from Freddy's house at 5 a.m., she had stayed up another hour to read Bert's notebook, to try and work out how to activate Dad Droid. This meant she had slept for a total of forty-three minutes. Normally, she had a proper lie-in on a Saturday, but not today.

She peered out and saw her father at the end of the drive, looking on as a man hammered a sign on a wooden post into the ground. Her mother poked her head round the bedroom door.

'Oh, you're awake, darling,' she said. 'How are you feeling?'

'What's going on out there? Who's that man?' asked Minnie.

'That's Mr Finton, darling. The estate agent.'

Just then the man twisted the sign around and Minnie could see it said, 'FOR SALE'.

She opened her mouth to say something but nothing came out.

'We have to sell the house I'm afraid, darling,' her mum said. 'But don't worry. Everything will work out fine. Probably. I mean it *might* not. But don't worry. Much.'

Minnie's mind started to race. They had always lived in this house! She couldn't leave her bedroom with its purple walls and purple carpet and purple chair and purple curtains and purple bed and orange cushion! And what about Freddy? What if they moved a hundred miles away and she couldn't see him any more? And what if she had to go to a different school where they made you eat cabbage every day and had a uniform with fluorescent piping and a horrible emblem of a grinning pig or something? – Her mind was *really* racing now.

'I'll make some breakfast,' her mother said and slipped out.

Minnie looked down to see Mr Finton, a grinny man with big teeth, shaking her dad's hand, then crossing to his car. As it drove off, her father tested the 'FOR SALE' sign to see if it wobbled, but it didn't. He shuffled up the path towards the house, looking more upset than ever.

Minnie was about to get down from her perch at the window when she spotted two figures marching down the street, heading straight for Freddy's house. It was Mr and

Miss Dribb, the people from P.O.O.F.A.C.E.! They were walking exactly in time, left, right, left, right, their highly polished glasses catching the sun and making them look fiery-eyed.

Minnie grabbed her *Ear to Ear* from a box under the bed, shot into the bathroom and buzzed Freddy.

There was no reply. All she could hear crackling through the speaker in her ear was 'Monkey in Me Bathtub' by Uncle Oony's Orchestra, blaring from the sound system in Freddy's house.

'Freddy! Wake up!' she shouted into the ear. 'RED ALERT!'

Doopy-doopy-do, doopy-do, doopy-do, went the band, while Uncle Oony sang in his raspy voice:

Da Monkey's in me barf again,
It's really hard to cope!
It's dancing on me hot tap
It's nibbling me soap!

She turned off the ear and looked out of the window again. Briefcases swinging in time, the Dribbs were now crossing the street. Although still in her pyjamas, Minnie shot downstairs and ran to the front gate. She leaned on the 'FOR SALE' sign, trying to look cool.

'Come to see the Birds?' she called out as the Dribbs walked past.

Mr Dribb sniffed coldly, his hand poised on Freddy's gate. 'Yes, small girl,' he said in his nasal voice. 'So what if we have?'

Minnie shrugged. 'Just that they're not in.' She looked at her nails, pretending to pick them with her thumb.

Miss Dribb stiffened and her neck gave a little crack. 'Where are they?'

'They've gone out for the day. To see an aunt.' Minnie tried to think up a fake story, fast. 'Aunt Flower… Bush. She's very ill, apparently. She's lost the use of her… nose.'

'What?'

'Yes, it's a very rare condition,' Minnie went on, 'called…'

She scanned round for inspiration and noticed a baker's lorry going by with 'HOBB'S BREAD' on the side of it.

'Hobb's Nostril.'

'Hobb's Nostril?!' Mr Dribb exclaimed.

'Yes. It was discovered by a Dr Hobb. He was a very clever doctor. Of noses, mainly.'

Mr Dribb's whole body clenched in disgust and he sucked air in through his teeth. 'When will they be back?'

'They didn't say,' said Minnie.

Miss Dribb scowled at Mr Dribb. 'If they're not in, there's no point trying, Dilbert. Let's come back later.'

Mr Dribb scraped Freddy's gate shut, angrily.

'Bye,' said Minnie. 'Have a nice day.'

'Huh!' said Mr Dribb.

She watched them march off in unison. They were holding their heads so high in the air, as if trying to avoid a bad smell, that they didn't see the end of the pavement, and both tripped up.

Minnie's mum appeared in the doorway. 'What are you doing out there in your pyjamas, Minither? Get dressed at once! We're going to look at some new houses. Well, not so much *houses*, more *flats*. One's a shed, actually. But don't worry. Everything will be all right. Probably. Although it might not.'

After her mum had gone in again, Minnie hurried next door and tapped on Freddy's window. The curtains parted and Freddy looked out, bleary-eyed. He pulled the window open.

'The Dribbs were here!' said Minnie. 'I managed to get rid of them but they're coming back!'

Freddy's eyes widened in panic. 'What am I going to do? I have to get the droid working!'

'According to the notebook, there's a red cable connected to its heart, which needs a massive surge of power to start it.'

'But where am I going to get that?' groaned Freddy.

'Minnie? Minither?!' Her mother's voice rang out.

'I've got to go! They're making me go with them to look at houses!'

Before Freddy could say anything, Minnie darted off.

He pulled the curtains back, letting light flood into the room, and stared down at Dad Droid in the chair. It was leaning forward like it was searching for something on the carpet. He heaved it back into a sitting position and Bert's gentle, if somewhat rubbery, features gazed up at him. The mouth was hanging open like he was about to burst into song. Pulling its clothes off, to see the machinery better, Freddy found a thick red cable sticking out of the droid's chest, ending in a clump of copper wires.

'Power… where can I find power?' Freddy racked his brain, scanning the room. He noticed the clock ticking on the wall. 'Of course!' He pulled it down and emptied out its batteries.

Then he ran through the house looking for anything with a battery in it: TV remotes, radios, the electric carving knife, even tiny ones from watches and other gadgets. He managed to haul in several incredibly heavy car batteries from the shed outside and ended up with over a hundred of all shapes and sizes, scattered across the floor. It took a while to link them all together, but at last he was holding the red cable from the droid's heart in one hand and the shaggy end of a long wire in the other, connected to the batteries.

'Please! Make this work,' he said, closing his eyes and willing with all his might.

He touched the wires together. With a loud buzz, Dad Droid jolted upright in the chair and its eyes clicked open.

Freddy began bounding round excitedly. 'I did it! He's awake! Ha ha ha ha ha!'

Then the droid bleated like some sort of electronic sheep, '*BERRRRRRRRR...!*' and slumped back.

The power went dead. Freddy felt like bursting into tears.

Just at that moment Timmy came floating downstairs. He had been in a sulk since Bert had gone missing but now, seeing the droid in the chair for the first time, his feline features crinkled into a smile. He thought Freddy's dad had come back.

'Miaow!'

With a firm push of his hind legs against the wall, he piloted his airship across the room and landed in the droid's lap. The cable from its robotic heart was dangling lifelessly from its chest and Timmy plonked straight onto it. There was a terrific blast from the electrically charged cat. Freddy almost fell backwards in surprise as the room lit up electric-blue.

'*MIAAAAAOOOOWWWW!*' squealed Timmy.

Sparks shot up the cable into the droid's artificial heart, bringing cogs and pistons to life. Blinding electricity spidered outwards in different directions through its body – down its legs and arms and up into its head, where for a moment the eyes gleamed like headlights and all the little diodes in its brain circuits blinked on.

Timmy's pink ears went flat to his skull and he shot from the room as Dad Droid sprang from the chair onto its metal feet, and shouted: 'BERRRRRRRRRRT! My name is BERRRRRT!'

Dad Droid was alive!

12

BERRRRRRRRRRRRT!

After his initial excitement had died down, the first thing that struck Freddy about Dad Droid was how unlike his dad it actually was. It might *look* like him but it didn't talk like him, or walk like him, or know anything about Freddy. In fact, it didn't even know who Freddy was.

At first the droid just lurched from room to room with clumpy steps, following him round and knocking things over.

'BERRRRT! BERRRRT!' it kept repeating in an echoey voice.

'That's right. Your name is Bert and you're my father. Sort of. And I'm Freddy. I'm your son – in a way. Not really, because you're a robot – it's hard to explain.'

Freddy caught a lamp as the droid sent it flying off a table with a sweep of his arm.

'BERRRRRRRRT! BERRRRRRRT! FARRRRRR-THER!'

'Oh, dear,' Freddy muttered.

'OH, DEARRRRRRRR!' the droid repeated, marching to the window and turning round in circles, and getting tangled in the curtains. With a ripping sound, the curtains and the rail crashed to the ground. Somehow Freddy managed to get Dad Droid across the room and sit it down, with the curtains still wrapped round it like a cloak.

'I'm going to have to train you,' said Freddy. 'You have to learn to be just like my dad. You see, there are these people called the Dribbs. They'll take me away if they think he's not looking after me. Do you understand?'

The droid swivelled its head in a full circle like some sort of crazed owl and smiled at Freddy, showing all its teeth.

'No! You mustn't do that! Especially when we have visitors,' said Freddy. 'It looks weird.'

The droid whirred as if taking in this information.

'Weird, yes, Freddink. Thank you, Freddink,' it said.

'And it's *Freddy*, not Freddink. F-R-E-D-D-Y.'

The droid gave a slow nod of its head but its eyes looked blank.

'Okay, let's start with your voice,' said Freddy.

'I have thirty-seven speech modes,' said the droid and went through a series of garbled voices, from the high warbling of an opera singer to the bark of a gruff army general.

'No!' said Freddy, blocking his ears. 'Stop! Stop!'

The droid went silent and looked at him, rather hurt.

Freddy caught sight of his father's *Voice-Translation System* on the table. 'I know; listen to this! This is what you have to sound like,' he said and switched on the machine.

'*Would you like some potatoes with your omelette?*' came his dad's voice through the speaker.

'Now *you* try,' said Freddy.

'*Would you like some potatoes with your omelette?*' the droid repeated in a harsh metallic voice.

'Deeper,' said Freddy. 'And with more feeling. Try again.'

'*Would you like some potatoes with your omelette?*' said the droid – and this time it didn't sound quite so mechanical.

'Good,' said Freddy. 'Much better.'

He sat back and watched as Dad Droid listened to the machine, repeating everything Bert said, like it was learning a foreign language. The more it practised, the more it tuned into Bert's pitch and tone until finally, when it said, 'How much is that bunch of carrots?' it sounded just like his dad.

'That's it! You've got it!' said Freddy, excited.

The droid sat forward and leant heavily on the table. With a splitting sound, the wood cracked down the middle, sending them both into a heap on the floor.

Freddy let out a weary sigh.

*

To teach the droid some more about himself and his dad, Freddy decided to show it some of their home movies. So he sat Dad Droid down in his darkened bedroom and set up Bert's old film projector.

'This is us at the seaside,' he said, as the film appeared, projected on the wall.

The droid's face lit up in the flickery light as it watched Freddy, aged three, buried up to his neck in sand. Freddy's shoes were sticking out a long way in front of him as if he had impossibly long legs.

Dad Droid made a few electronic beeps as it processed what it was seeing. 'This means human children are much

taller when they're younger,' it concluded. 'Therefore, they shrink as they grow up.'

'No!' said Freddy, laughing. 'It's a joke! Look!'

Dad Droid ruffled its brow in thought as three-year-old Freddy got up, letting the sand fall off him. His shoes were still sticking out where they'd been buried.

The droid looked across at Freddy, taking in his laughter. 'What is that sound you're making?'

'I'm laughing,' said Freddy. 'It's what you do when something's funny.'

An odd noise rumbled from the droid's speech-box, like a lot of nails shaking round. It was trying to laugh but its face was still set in a serious expression.

'No, Dad Droid! You have to find something *funny* first. And it would help if you smiled,' said Freddy. He broke off, pointing at the film again: 'That's when we had a picnic in the woods,' he said. Projected on the wall, a slightly older Freddy was darting behind trees, hiding. His dad appeared on screen a moment later, searching for him. Again the droid was puzzled.

'Why are you hiding from your father?' it asked. 'Are you afraid of him?'

'No, it's a game called Hide and Seek.'

The droid shook its head. 'I do not understand. What is the purpose of this "game"?'

'It's fun!'

'Fun?'

'Yes! It makes you happy!' said Freddy.

Dad Droid groaned and its brain made loud clicking noises as it struggled to make sense of this.

'Oh, there's too much to explain!' Freddy sighed. 'How am I going to teach you all these things?'

After four or five more films, Freddy switched off the projector and let the sunlight back into the room.

Dad Droid stood up and crossed to a bookshelf. It pulled out a book with its metallic fingers, flicked it open and started to scan the words. It took under a second for the droid to read each page, and soon it was leafing through the book so fast Freddy could hardly see anything through the blur of movement. In under a minute the droid dropped the book, which was *David's Magic Toast, Book 15, The Deadly Jam of Death.*

'What are you doing?' said Freddy.

'Learning,' said Dad Droid, scanning through *The Horrible Adventures of Doctor Ong.* 'About castles and mirrors and mountains and beards and dragons.' Its eyes were bright with excitement, seeing the world for the first time through these stories.

Freddy darted across to his bed where an encyclopedia was propping up the wobbly leg. He thrust it into Dad Droid's hands. It was part one of ten huge volumes.

'Read this. It'll tell you everything,' said Freddy.

Dad Droid turned to page one: 'Aardvark: a nocturnal burrowing mammal native to Africa.'

All kinds of expressions passed over the droid's face as it raced through the encyclopedia, taking in images and information at an impossible speed:

Albert Einstein…

The Flight of the Common Bat…

How to make a Victoria Sponge…

The History of Sandals…

Dad Droid's memory banks were filling up, fast. Freddy hauled down the other nine encyclopedias and piled them next to the robot.

'When you've finished that, read these,' he said.

'Yes, yes, Freddy,' said the droid impatiently, just the way Bert did when you disturbed him.

His plan was going to work! The droid was already much more like his father and soon its mind would be overflowing with facts and figures just like his dad's!

KNOCK-KNOCK-KNOCK!

Freddy shot to his feet. 'Someone's at the door!'

Dad Droid looked up from memorising a map of Norway. They heard the front door creak open.

'Anybody here?'… 'Hello?' Two whiny voices echoed up from the hallway.

The Dribbs were back!

13

FLYING SUGAR LUMPS

Freddy ran to the banister and peered down. Mr and Miss Dribb were poking round the hallway, picking up bits of inventions and shaking their heads.

'I'm writing down "total utter mess",' Miss Dribb sneered, scribbling on her clipboard.

'I've put "total utter *utter* mess",' said Mr Dribb.

Freddy crept back to the droid and whispered: 'Now remember, you're my dad. Your name is Bert Bird. You have to shake their hands and offer them some tea.'

'T? I do not understand. I will offer them a letter from the alphabet?'

'No. "Tea". T-E-A.' Freddy opened the encyclopaedia to an entry about it. 'Quick! Read this!'

As the droid was scanning the page, Freddy steeled himself and went down.

'There you are, boy,' said Mr Dribb. 'Where's your father? We need to speak to him immediately.'

'Sooner, if possible,' snapped Miss Dribb.

Freddy called up: 'Dad? There's some people to see you.'

His heart started to beat fast and he felt his face go very hot as he heard the droid thump across the landing. The moment it appeared, Freddy realised he had forgotten to put the fake-skin coverings over its metal hands.

'There you are, Dad,' he said, darting in front of the droid, pulling the flesh-coloured gloves into place.

Mr Dribb looked suspicious, trying to see what Freddy was up to. 'Is something wrong? What are you doing?'

'Nothing,' said Freddy. 'Now shake their hands!' he whispered to the droid. 'And try to act normal.'

Dad Droid advanced on Miss Dribb and took both her hands, shaking them up and down very fast, like it was beginning some sort of dance.

'What are you doing?' said Miss Dribb angrily. 'Let go of me!'

'It's just his little joke,' said Freddy. He tried to laugh but no one was finding it funny.

The droid let go of Miss Dribb, who fell backwards into the hatstand, a bowler hat and several scarves landing on top of her.

As she was getting up, muttering crossly, Dad Droid turned to shake Mr Dribb's hands the same way, but he recoiled. '*Mr Bird!*' he barked, 'you must take this seriously!'

The droid looked panicked and, unsure what to say,

blurted out the first phrase it had ever learnt. '*Would you like some potatoes with your omelette?*'

'What are you talking about? What omelette?' said Mr Dribb.

Behind the Dribbs' backs, Freddy started mouthing 'Tea' to the droid and pointing to the kitchen.

'Ah! I will prepare some tea!' said Dad Droid and headed towards the kitchen door, which was closed.

Freddy raced to stop it, realising he hadn't taught the droid to open doors yet. But it was too late. Dad Droid smashed through the wood, leaving a man-size hole in it.

The Dribbs looked at each other in horror, then began scribbling frantically on their clipboards.

'I'm putting "Situation Urgent",' said Miss Dribb.

'I'm putting "Situation *Really* Urgent",' said Mr Dribb. 'In red.'

'Of course it's red! *And* I'm underlining it.'

'I'm underlining it *twice*!'

'You've never done that before!'

'It's never been this *urgent* before!'

'Wait,' said Freddy, 'I can explain. My Dad's a bit unusual, that's all. It doesn't mean he can't look after me. Look, here he comes now with some lovely tea.'

Freddy gestured to where Dad Droid was emerging through the hole in the kitchen door, carrying a teapot.

'May I offer you some tea?' it said and, before the

Dribbs could answer, started pouring it, mid-air, splashing it all over their clipboards.

'You forgot the cups!' Freddy shouted.

All the horrible things the Dribbs had been writing down washed off their papers. Boiling hot tea, mixed with black and red ink, dripped over their toes, making them hop round in circles.

'Ow!'

'Ouch!'

'My shoes!'

'My feet!'

'Milk?' asked Dad Droid, lobbing a carton at its guests.

Miss Dribb ducked just in time as it smashed against the wall.

'He's mad!' she shrieked. 'No child can live in a house like this! Let's get out of here!'

'Sugar?' Dad Droid continued.

Freddy looked on open-mouthed as the Dribbs hurtled down the path with sugar lumps firing at their backs. Milk had splashed all over Miss Dribb's glasses and she couldn't see properly so she was veering all over the place, knocking over flowerpots and bouncing off shrubs.

'Thanks for coming,' Dad Droid called after them in Bert's chirpy voice as they scurried down the street as fast as their legs could carry them.

Dad Droid turned to Freddy. 'Oh,' it said, 'I forgot to offer them a biscuit.'

Freddy looked devastated. 'You've just made everything much worse!' he screamed. 'Didn't those books teach you anything?'

The droid's brain circuits clicked into action. 'Yes,' it said. 'Sunflowers can grow to a height of four hundred centimetres.'

'It's not *facts* you need, it's *manners*!' Freddy snapped.

'I am detecting anger signals from you, Freddy,' said

the droid. 'Your pulse rate is increasing and your voice has raised in volume.'

Freddy pulled some more books from the bookcase and pushed the droid into a chair, thrusting them into its arms. 'Read these,' he said. 'Maybe these'll teach you to be more… more human.'

The droid read the covers. '*How to be Polite. The A–Z of Etiquette.* Interesting.'

'And don't move till you've finished!' said Freddy.

The droid looked at him quizzically. 'But Freddy, if I can't move, how can I turn the pages?'

'You can move *your hands*!' Freddy growled, exasperated. 'I need a break. I'm going out to get some air!'

The sound of the front door slamming echoed through the house. The droid shook its head. 'Humans say some funny things sometimes.' It opened both books at once and began to scan them at the same time.

*

Freddy had just turned the corner at the end of the street when, unseen by him, Miss Arbourteel came round the corner at the opposite end. She had been restless all weekend, thinking about Freddy and his encounter with the Dribbs at school. It was her fault they'd come to investigate him and she felt more and more guilty about contacting them. No matter what she did, her mind kept wandering back to Freddy till she could take it no more and decided to call round. Her hand was still on the knocker when the front door opened and she was met by Freddy's dad, smiling warmly.

'Oh! Mr Bird!' she said, surprised. Thinking back to the last time she'd been there and overheard his phone call, she added: 'I thought you were in Morocco.'

'Morocco? Population 33.8 million,' said the droid.

'Really? *Très intéressant!*'

'Ah, you are French! – *Tu es français!*' said the droid in a perfect accent. In the six minutes since Freddy had left, Dad Droid had finished both the books it had been given and moved on to all the others it could find, including a complete French language course. It began to discuss the weather and make small talk in fluent French.

Forgetting why she'd come, Miss Arbourteel blushed and prodded her bun, enchanted. Mr Bird seemed to have impeccable manners and his knowledge of Paris was extraordinary. She began to giggle coyly like she did in class when she was describing the lovely times Chantelle and Jerome shared together (before he went suddenly to Belgium).

She was smitten.

*

Freddy's walk had taken him twice round the park by which time he'd calmed down from his frustration with the droid. The past few days had been exhausting and emotional. He felt like he'd grown up ten years.

But as he started to head home, he began to feel on edge again. He had the strong sensation he was being followed and kept glancing behind, but there was no one there. A few moments later, however, he heard a low growl and felt a warm sensation on the back of his legs. Mr Wortnall's shark-car had come up behind him out of nowhere.

The rear window buzzed down – fully this time – and Wortnall appeared, lit up by the lights inside the car. He had a clammy, chalk-white face, white hair and piercing ratty eyes. As before he was puffing on a foul-smelling cigar.

'So, Er-er-er-Freddy, we meet again.'

Freddy looked up and saw a crowbot hovering in the fug around the car. The mechanical bird fluttered down and perched on the roof. Its electronic eye glinted as the camera lens zoomed in on him.

'That's right. I used my little friend here to track you down,' said Wortnall, gesturing up at the crowbot with his cigar.

'I have to go home. I'm late,' said Freddy, trying to get past.

'We weren't introduced before. My name is Mr C. G. Wortnall.'

Puff, puff.

Smoke from the cigar coiled around Freddy's neck. He coughed, choking on it.

'You're Bert Bird's boy, aren't you?' said Wortnall. 'What were you and your friend doing snooping round my factory?'

'Looking for my dad. Where is he? What's happened to him?'

Wortnall ignored him. 'I want his book,' he said.

'What book?'

'His *notebook*, boy. He's been working on a project for me for the last ten years. That book has everything I need in it and it belongs to me. Where is it?'

Minnie had taken the notebook to read up about the robot's power supply.

'I haven't got it,' said Freddy truthfully.

Mr Wortnall frowned, his pasty face sagging downwards.

'Think carefully, boy… *think*… *think* …'

Freddy found himself staring into Wortnall's hypnotic eyes. They had deep dark centres with lots of red veins in the white bits. He had to use all his concentration to drag himself away from them. 'I… don't know what you're talking about,' he stammered.

Wortnall sneered and sucked on his cigar, making the end glow fiery orange.

'Get in,' he said, opening the car door.

Freddy shook his head.

With a squawk the crowbot landed on the cobbles nearby and started hopping towards Freddy.

'You'd better be quick, boy.'

The crowbot's beak flopped open and a laser beam shot out, hitting the wall behind Freddy in a burst of sparks.

'GET IN!'

Another beam shot past Freddy, narrowly missing him. The crow jumped closer, head twisting from side to side as it tried to fix on its target. In one swift movement, Freddy punched the robotic bird with all his might, sending it flying into the back seat of the car in a cloud of synthetic feathers, straight into Wortnall's face. Mr Wortnall let out a shriek as the bird fluttered manically round him trying to get out.

'Sorry. Can't stay,' said Freddy, leaping onto the car bonnet, then over a wall, and dropping to the ground on the other side.

He ran as fast as he could, dodging through the narrow alleys that ran behind the houses, where the shark-car would be too wide to fit. Every few seconds he glanced back to check he wasn't being followed and looked up into the channel of sky between the brick walls, in case of crowbots.

Reaching his front door, Freddy stopped in shock. It was already open, the door frame splintered where it had been kicked in. Cautiously, he stepped inside.

The house was wrecked. Furniture, clothes and objects lay smashed and torn everywhere. Timmy was hovering in a corner, mewing in fright. Freddy tried to calm him.

'Dad Droid?' he whispered, tiptoeing through the house with Timmy at his shoulder. 'Dad Droid, where are you?'

There was a boom from the floor above. Freddy jumped back as a bedside cabinet was thrown down, smashing to bits at the bottom of the stairs. Footsteps thudded above, accompanied by gruff voices. Freddy's heart began to pound. Someone was ripping the house apart!

The footsteps grew louder. They were heading his way!

Freddy leapt into the coats hanging by the door, pulling them over him. He peered out to see two lumbering figures looming into view.

It was Mr Wortnall's henchmen, Peek and Troff.

14

THE RED NOTEBOOK

'What we lookin' for again?' grunted Mr Peek.

'A red notebook, you idiot!' Mr Troff kicked over a table with a vase on it, for emphasis.

'I've found this *yellow* one.' Peek held up a book.

'Well, that's not it then, is it!'

'No. I s'pose not.'

Freddy ducked back between the coats and slid his feet into his dad's wellies, as they threw objects round, searching.

'We've already looked down 'ere.'

'Well, look again! If we go back without that book, Wortnall will put us back on toilet duty.'

'I hate filthy loos,' moaned Peek.

'Then look harder!'

There was a sudden beeping sound. Troff pressed his watch. Wortnall's creepy white face beamed out from it on a little screen.

'Have you found the red notebook?' he snapped.

'Not really, sir,' said Troff.

'What do you mean, "not really"?'

'I found a *yellow* one!' said Mr Peek hopefully.

'Shut up!' Troff hissed, elbowing him.

Wortnall sneered. 'Listen, you meatheads: if that boy comes back, grab him as well. See what he's done to me. He threw a crowbot in my face. I've got a claw-mark down my little cheek now!' He pointed to a cut on his clammy skin. 'Keep looking till you find that book!'

'Yes, boss. Yeah.'

The screen on the watch went dead.

Freddy slithered further along the line of coats. He had to get out without them seeing him. He heard a miaow. Timmy was wafting above, trying to get his attention. It was past his suppertime and he was hungry.

Troff swung round, staring at the cat. 'What's that stupid creature up to?'

'Yuck. I hate cats,' said Peek. ''Specially flying ones.'

Troff and Peek came right over so they were standing an armslength from Freddy. He stayed as still as he could, not daring to move a muscle. 'I'll get rid of it,' said Peek, snatching an umbrella in his hairy hand. He lunged forward, jabbing the cat with the metal spike. The moment it touched Timmy, sparks from the electrified animal ran down the umbrella, along Peek's arm and lit up his whole body like an X-ray, so you could see his skeleton. He was thrown back with the most enormous jolt as the electric shock ran through him.

'AAAAAAAGH!'

Troff couldn't help laughing.

'Wretched animal!' Peek cursed, picking himself up. His clothes were steaming and his eyebrows were singed. The shock also made Timmy's airship burst, releasing him from his harness for the first time in weeks. Disorientated to find himself plonked back on solid ground, he scuttled a few steps, then keeled over with a growl.

Peek hurled the brolly after him, missing him by a whisker.

'Leave it, Peek! Come on! We've got to keep looking!'

Troff stepped so close to the coat rack that he actually trod on the wellies Freddy was standing in. Freddy had to bite the coat hanging in front of him to stifle a yelp. He sat tight in his hiding place while Troff and Peek continued pulling the house apart. The longer they searched, the more annoyed they got, till they were thumping one another instead of looking for the notebook.

At last, when Freddy's legs were beginning to go numb from being stuck in the same position, Troff and Peek came back into the hallway, looking dejected.

'Think how angry Mr Wortnall's going to be!' Peek moaned.

'Oh, shut up,' said Troff, giving him a shove.

'We've looked everywhere! It's not here! Let's go!'

'No,' Troff grunted. 'He said we have to wait till the brat comes back and nab him, so we're stuck 'ere, aren't we?!'

They pulled open the fridge and took out everything they could find. Then they slumped in front of the TV and started guzzling, only breaking off to argue and thump each other every so often.

It wasn't long before they were surrounded by discarded packaging and had fallen asleep, snoring and belching, with the TV blaring out *WHERE'S GRANNY?* (A popular game show in which contestants have to search for camouflaged old ladies.)

Freddy slipped out of his hiding place and crept upstairs. He glanced in every room, but the droid wasn't there. It looked like an earthquake had struck the house, wherever Troff and Peek had been. He grabbed a rucksack from his bedroom and shoved all the essentials he thought he might need into it – clothes, a torch, his penknife, a map of the area – then went downstairs to get more supplies.

While he was piling what was left in the kitchen cupboards into his bag, he caught sight of the statue in the back garden. Maybe Dad Droid had gone to hide in the secret tunnel, to get away from Wortnall's henchmen?

Freddy crept out, scrambled through the undergrowth, hauled the chubby cupid aside and shone his torch down the hole.

'Dad Droid?' he called, in a harsh whisper. 'Are you down there?'

He climbed down the metal ladder to the bottom of the pipe, where his torch lit up an empty tunnel.

Turning back to the ladder, he froze as a trickle of soil fell on him from above. There were clanging sounds.

Someone was climbing down!

He clicked off his torch and crouched in the darkness. Peek and Troff must have woken up and spotted him creeping into the garden! He was trapped!

As the sound of clanging feet got louder, moving down the metal rungs, Freddy raised his torch, ready to strike. A pool of spreading light grew at the bottom of the ladder as the intruder's torch got closer. Freddy took a step forward, aiming his weapon.

'AAAAAGH!' Minnie screamed, as she stepped off the ladder and saw Freddy coming at her.

'AAAAAGH!' screamed Freddy.

The two children stopped, facing each other.

'What are *you* doing here?' Freddy spluttered.

'I've run away,' said Minnie, who was also wearing a backpack. 'You should see the place my parents want to move to. It's on the other side of town next to the Sewage Works. It's horrible. Why are *you* here?'

'Looking for Dad Droid,' said Freddy. 'He's gone missing. And now Wortnall's after me. His thugs are in the house looking for the red notebook.

Minnie patted her bag. 'Don't worry. I haven't let it out of my sight.'

As they climbed back up the ladder, she noticed Freddy's rucksack. 'Where are you going?'

He glanced back at her, more determined than ever. 'Back to the factory. I have to find out what happened to my dad.'

'I'm coming too,' Minnie said without missing a beat.

*

Moments later they were creeping down the alleyway between their two houses.

As they emerged onto the pavement, Minnie's front door burst open and her father ran out. 'MINNIE! MINNIE, COME BACK THIS INSTANT!' he shouted after her. Her mother ran out too in floods of tears, brandishing a piece of paper.

'Oh, no! They've found my note!' said Minnie.

'Why did you leave a *note*?' Freddy groaned.

'You *have* to leave a note when you run away.'

'Come on!' He took Minnie's hand and they sprinted as fast as they could down the street.

Mrs Carstairs shrieked, pushing her husband down the path, 'SHE'S WITH THAT BIRD BRAT! STOP THEM, DONALD!'

The children skidded to a halt as a huge grey van, with

the initials P.O.O.F.A.C.E. on the side, pulled up in front of them. Mr and Miss Dribb jumped out.

'There he is!' said Mr Dribb, narrowing his eyes. 'Get the net!'

'It's for your own good!' snapped Miss Dribb, trying to grab Freddy's collar.

Woken by the commotion, Peek and Troff lumbered onto the street just in time to see a small boy and girl darting from the clutches of a flustered middle-aged couple and two people in suits waving a huge net.

'That's the boy!' shouted Peek.

'GET HIM!' Troff screamed.

Freddy and Minnie ducked and dived as hands grabbed at them from all directions. Eventually, they managed to slip free and at the end of the road, with the mob at their heels, Freddy shouted: 'This way!' and pulled Minnie up the path between the snooty stone lions, straight through the front door of posh Mrs Crumley's house.

Mrs Crumley was perched on a gold settee, sipping a small glass of sherry, with Randolph, her pink-permed poodle, on her lap, talking to a very skinny woman with a long face like a horse. 'Yeeeeeessssss, Lady Troot-Williams, it is *such* a peaceful neighbourhood,' she was saying just as Freddy and Minnie ran through the lounge, heading for the back garden, knocking over a cut-glass-crystal water feature on the way.

A split second later, six people stampeded through

the room, between the two shocked ladies, trampling mud into the Persian carpet and smashing ornaments, before disappearing after the children through the French windows.

Mrs Crumley sat with her once-perfect *Lola-Fringe* looking like an explosion in a wig factory. She was too well-bred to even mention what had just happened. 'Would you care for some more sherry?' she asked weakly.

*

Freddy and Minnie vaulted over the beautifully trimmed hedges – in the shape of swans and peacocks – at the end of Mrs Crumley's garden and kept running. There was a loud miaow. Timmy had followed them from the house and was scampering along the wall beside them, trying to keep up. With one great bound he landed on Freddy's rucksack and dug his claws in, to hold on.

'They're catching up!' cried Minnie.

Some of the adults had clicked their *You-Shoes* up to maximum speed and now their *La-di-das* and *Superstacks* and *Gavins* were propelling them faster and faster.

'Jump on my shoes again!' Freddy shouted to Minnie.

As Minnie held on tight, Freddy turned his *Gavins* to 'DASH!' and they whizzed off.

It was quite a sight! The children and the mob pursuing them caused major disruption when they reached the high street. Cars and buses had to swerve out of the way. They knocked people's shopping from their arms and upturned rubbish bins.

The children turned a corner onto a side street and came to an abrupt halt outside a café. Freddy's mind was working fast. 'If we can wind our way round to the park, we can escape across the golf course…' But Minnie wasn't listening.

'Freddy, look!' she shouted, staring in disbelief through the café window. 'It's Dad Droid!'

At a table in the window, Dad Droid was sitting opposite Miss Arbourteel, treating her to dinner. The *A–Z of Etiquette*, which Freddy had left the robot reading, had made it clear that it was polite for gentlemen to ask out eligible single ladies and make intelligent conversation. Miss Arbourteel looked much softer and less teachery than she did at school.

They had been talking for an hour, in perfect French, about music, art and the recipes for various delicious pastries, which Dad Droid had gleaned from various books in its memory banks. Miss Arbourteel's silvery laugh trickled and she blushed like a girl, toying with the prawns on her plate. She had never expected to meet anyone who made her feel special again, after losing Jerome all those years before.

Dad Droid was describing a walk along the River Seine it had memorised from a travel guide: 'And, of course, if you look left you see the beautiful façade of Notre Dame Cathedral, built in 1163…'

Miss Arbourteel's romantic past in Paris came flooding back. 'Excuse me a moment. I'm just going to powder my

nose,' she said and trotted off to the bathroom, quite overcome with emotion.

Just then the crowd chasing the two children turned the corner onto the side street. With no time to lose, Freddy ran in and grabbed Dad Droid's arm. 'Come on. We've got to go!'

He dragged the robot through the restaurant into the kitchens. As they rushed past, the chef dropped his ladle in the soup, splashing green liquid everywhere. Seconds later, the Dribbs, Mr and Mrs Carstairs, Peek and Troff, as well as a whole stream of other angry people who had been knocked into or tripped up by the children, smashed through the kitchen sending '*Seared Chicken on a Bed of Spicy Couscous*' flying.

Meanwhile, Miss Arbourteel returned from the Ladies, breathless with romance, to find her table upturned and the head waiter hurrying towards her with the bill.

'*Mon Dieu*,' she whimpered, sinking onto her chair. 'Not again! It's just like Jerome. Gone... *gone*!'

*

By the time Freddy, Minnie, Dad Droid and Timmy reached the golf course on the edge of town, it was getting late and the moon was darting in and out of the clouds.

'Head for those woods!' said Freddy, as they jumped across a sandy bunker near the eighteenth hole. 'We can lose them in there!'

The pine trees ahead looked thick and dark, just the sort of place to shake off their pursuers.

'It looks spooky,' cried Minnie.

'We've got no choice,' said Freddy.

Most of the crowd chasing them had fallen behind, but Troff and Peek were still bumbling along like sweaty pigs, aware of the punishment that awaited them if they returned empty-handed.

'Our average speed is 12 miles per hour,' said Dad Droid calmly, as they ran. 'We should reach the trees in

39.7 seconds.' Being a robot, it was never out of breath and didn't seem aware of any danger.

39.7 seconds later, they disappeared into the woods.

15

THE CAPITAL CITY OF OYSTER

'Where are we going?' asked Minnie in a hushed voice.

'I don't know. We're lost,' said Freddy, marching on in a dark mood.

Dad Droid stomped between them, carrying Timmy. The droid was generating a fair amount of heat and the exhausted cat had curled up and gone to sleep in its arms.

By now they had been walking for hours through the woods. The trees seemed to get thicker and blacker the further they went, till there were just tiny patches of night sky showing through the branches above. The stars looked cold and sharp piercing down. It was starting to get cold and the wind made the trees creak and groan eerily.

'Can't we stop?' said Minnie.

'No. We have to keep going,' said Freddy. 'What if they're still following?'

'Would you like me to recite some poetry, to pass the

time?' Dad Droid suggested and, without waiting for a reply, scanned through the data in its brain till it found something suitable. '*'Twas dismal in the dreaded wood, where fear and awful danger lurked—*'

'NO!' both children said at once.

'No poetry,' said Freddy sternly.

'Oh,' said the robot. 'How about a song then?' Again, without waiting for an answer, it blared out: '*It's a horrible nasty awful dangerous night, And the monsters in the trees are just out of sight—*'

Freddy clamped a hand over the droid's mouth.

'No singing either! We don't want anyone to hear us. Don't you understand? We're escaping. We're on the run.'

'Oh. We are in *danger*, are we?' Dad Droid enquired innocently.

'Yes,' said Freddy, trying to be patient. 'Didn't you notice all those people running after us?'

'I assumed they were engaged in some sort of sports activity,' said the droid, 'But now I understand. Thank you for explaining, Freddy. I will update my information.'

Freddy's torch, which he had been shining into the undergrowth in front, suddenly dipped to a flicker. Then, a few steps later, it went out.

'We've *got* to stop now, Freddy,' said Minnie. 'It's too dark to see. We could trip over something any minute and – AAAAAAGH!'

There was a thump, some rolling noises and a splash.

'Minnie! Where are you?' Freddy squinted into the darkness. 'Are you all right? – MINNIE!'

'Down here!'

She had fallen down a slope into a stinky pond. Freddy scrambled down and hauled her out. She was dripping wet. You could hear her feet squelch in her shoes with every step and she now smelt like an old drain. She fished in her pocket and brought out a soggy packet of Minty Double-Chockshocks as they trudged on.

'Great!' she said. 'They're ruined.'

'It's all right. I've got some food in my rucksack.'

'Not Minty Double-Chockshocks, though,' she grumbled.

Not long after that they reached the edge of the wood and found themselves in open countryside. Across a stretch of heath, they could make out the distant outline of more trees.

'What do we do? Go back or go across?' said Minnie. She was hoping Freddy would decide to turn round, so they could find somewhere to stop for the night. But something kept driving him on. 'Let's cross to the other side,' he said with determination.

Halfway across the expanse of rabbit-nibbled grass and heather, there was a rumble from the skies.

'Oh, no.' Freddy looked up.

Clouds were rolling across the moon. A drop of rain splatted onto his upturned face. Then, a second

BUZZ
SPARK!

later, the heavens opened and a torrential downpour pelted from the sky as if someone had turned on a massive tap.

'Doesn't bother me. I'm soaked already,' said Minnie.

'It's not you I'm worried about!' Freddy snapped. 'Look at Dad Droid!'

Smoke was hissing from the droid's left ear and its eyes were rolling round like some kind of out-of-control fruit machine.

'Quick! We've got to keep him dry!' Freddy said, throwing his coat over the droid's head.

'The Capital city of Oyster is 0.732,' said Dad Droid in the voice of a young woman. Sparks erupted in its mouth, making its teeth light up.

'The rain's getting into his circuits. We've got to get him undercover!' Freddy said.

Holding their coats over it like an umbrella, the children bundled Dad Droid across the heath.

'How many eels are there on that bicycle?' said Dad Droid, in a thick Scottish accent. Its head turned back to front, while the rest of him continued facing forwards.

'It's all right, Dad Droid,' said Freddy. 'We'll be under those trees in a minute.'

The droid suddenly stood very upright and jerked its arms apart, adopting a ballet pose. 'Position 5!'

Timmy the cat was sent flying from its arms into a

gorse bush. He sprang up with an angry glare and began darting alongside.

'What's happening to him?' Minnie said.

'He's malfunctioning. We have to keep his mind focused.' Freddy turned to the droid: 'Remember you're *Bert Bird.* You're my *father.* Sort of.'

'Berrrrrrrrt,' Dad Droid repeated, just like it had when it was first switched on.

'That's right!' said Freddy.

Minnie took its hand. 'Remember Miss Arbourteel,' she said.

Dad Droid's automated smile curved upwards as it remembered their candlelit dinner. But then, almost at once, it stopped dead and the smile faded. 'System error! I did not pay for the meal! Chapter 3, Line 7, *The A–Z of Etiquette*: *"The gentleman always pays for the lady!"* I must go back to Monsieur Bertrand's Café!' And it started marching back across the heath.

'It's too late!' Freddy turned Dad Droid round. 'Anyway, you don't have any money.'

'Money, a medium of exchange in the form of coins and potatoes.'

'Yes, that's *almost* right,' said Freddy.

Reaching the woods on the other side of the heath, they plunged once more into darkness. The smell of damp leaf mould and tree bark filled their nostrils. The rain beat deafeningly on the treetops like some great audience cheering and clapping. Trails of water glooped down the backs of their necks and up their sleeves. Minnie stumbled again, tripping over a root.

'I can't see *anything*!' she wailed.

'Would my internal mouth-torch be of use?' asked the droid, sounding more its old self.

A beam clicked on, shining from its mouth and lighting the path.

'You mean you had that all the time?' said Freddy, exasperated.

'Oh, yes,' said the droid.

'Why didn't you switch it on?'

'You didn't ask.'

Minnie slumped down against a tree. 'I can't walk any further. Can't we stop?'

'Shine your torch round, Dad Droid,' said Freddy. 'Let's see where we are.'

A few feet away, the beam lit up a vast horse chestnut with branches trailing to the ground.

'Let's get under here,' Minnie suggested, crawling in.

It was quite snug under the leafy canopy and more or less waterproof. For a moment they sat in silence, listening to the rain, relieved to be resting their aching feet. Minnie took some clothes out of her bag and got changed. It felt much better to be dry again. Then Freddy brought out some bread and cheese, and they munched on that. Even Timmy had a nibble.

'Doesn't *he* need to eat?' said Minnie, pointing to Dad Droid.

'Only electricity,' said Freddy. Dad Droid was leaning against the tree, emitting a low hum.

As they watched, its eyes started to pulse with an amber light.

'What's he doing?' asked Freddy.

'I'll look it up,' said Minnie, fishing the notebook from her bag and leafing through it. 'According to this, he's in some sort of standby mode, to save energy.'

'In that case we should get some sleep as well,' said Freddy.

Minnie slipped the precious book back in her bag and used it as a pillow – that way nobody could get at it without her knowing. Freddy lay down next to her. The ground was lumpy and it took a lot of shifting round to get comfortable. Within minutes he could hear Minnie snoring. But although he was exhausted, Freddy couldn't get to sleep.

The rain pounded on. The wind rose and sent the trees swishing madly. He turned over but whichever way he lay, roots and stones dug into him. When he was younger, if he couldn't get to sleep he would find his dad, climb on his knee and rest his head against his chest so he could hear his heartbeat.

Freddy got up and went over to Dad Droid. He sat against it, reaching an arm around the robot's chest and looked up into Bert's gentle features, but they didn't move. The orange light just kept pulsing on and off in the droid's eyes. Its body wasn't soft and comfy like his dad's. He could feel its cold steel frame underneath the clothes. He sat up and shoved the droid away from him. 'You're not my dad! And you never will be!' he said.

He began to think about his father and his funny ways. He'd give anything to walk to school with him again, even if he *was* wearing odd shoes and a ladies' coat, because that was what made him his dad: eccentric, kind, brilliant. If only he could see him again, even for a few minutes, he could tell him how much he loved him.

It was then he noticed Dad Droid's eyes had stopped pulsing and begun to flicker instead. The faint sound of tinny voices and laughter was coming from somewhere inside it.

Freddy leant in close and stared into the droid's eyes.

It was like looking through binoculars. Inside its head, he could see blurred images of all the things Dad Droid had seen since Freddy had brought him to life, as if the robot was sorting through information. Beyond the orange glow, he saw himself and his dad on a sledge in the snow in one of their home movies. Then they were jumping down a sand dune. Now he saw himself in the back garden, sitting in the sunshine a few days after his mother had died. He remembered how upset he had been and how his dad had helped him through it. Somehow he always made things better, even the really bad things.

As he watched, the films got fainter and blurrier until the amber light went out altogether. The sounds of laughter and murmuring voices faded to nothing. All Freddy could see in the dark pupils of the droid's eyes was the reflection of his own small face with tears rolling down it.

As he lay down, watching the leaves thrash above him in the wind, he said to himself: 'I want him back! I want my dad!' For the first time Freddy thought the worst; he might never see his dad again. He was gone forever.

*

Soon after, when Freddy was finally asleep, something clicked inside the droid's head and a small green light blinked on in its neck.

As the children slept, Dad Droid got to its feet and walked off into the night.

16

DRIVE, DROID, DRIVE!

Freddy woke up to a kick in the shins. Sunlight was glittering through the canopy of leaves. Minnie was standing over him, looking shocked. Her hair was sticking up wildly and had twigs in it.

'He's gone!' she said.

Freddy sat bolt upright.

'Who has?'

'Dad Droid!'

Freddy leapt to his feet and pushed his way out of the hanging branches of the horse chestnut. Scanning the woods, all he could see were trees stretching into the distance, with yesterday's rainwater glistening on the greenery.

'We have to go after him.'

'How can we?' said Minnie. 'We don't know where he's gone.'

'But why would he leave? Unless someone took him?'

Freddy looked round with a shiver. Troff and Peek might be nearby.

'Look!'

Minnie pointed to a trail of footprints in the mud, leading off into the woods. Because Dad Droid was made of metal, its prints were deeper than any human's, so they would be easier to follow.

Grabbing their bags, they set off, following the trail. Timmy hopped into Freddy's rucksack, his face framed in the drawstrings, peering out. He had never been this far from home before and he was enjoying looking out at all the tasty woodland birds.

The woods were beautiful. Birdsong filled the morning air and the sun beamed dappled light through the treetops onto the forest floor. In places, wild flowers were growing in great clumps. In others, the huge fallen carcasses of trees lay like the limbs of dinosaurs.

'I wonder where we are,' said Minnie.

'Have a look.' Freddy pulled out his map and thrust it at her. As they strode on, she tried to trace their route from town, but the map was very large and kept flapping in her face or folding up.

They came to a dark valley of pines where there was suddenly less light. The birds were much quieter here. Neither of the children said anything to the other, but they both began to feel a creeping sensation, like a tingle at the back of the neck.

'I reckon we're here,' said Minnie, pointing to a dense patch of green on the map. It was miles from town. 'Or maybe here.' She pointed to more sprawling woodland in a completely different place. 'I'm not much good at map reading.'

'Sssh!' said Freddy, pulling her to a stop.

They listened.

After a moment there was a cracking sound, like a gun being cocked, ready to fire.

Minnie clutched Freddy's arm. A branch nearby creaked, then something thumped to the ground.

'What is it?' said Minnie in a breathless voice.

There were more cracking sounds and thuds all around them.

Then Minnie laughed, pointing. 'Pine cones!' she said.

Pine cones were cracking open in the sun and falling from the trees. Freddy let out a sigh of relief. 'How pathetic! Freaked out by a bunch of stupid pine cones!'

They went on again, dodging the grenade-shaped cones falling around them. Dad Droid's footprints were harder to follow over the carpet of pine needles, but eventually they reached a clearing and once again saw them leading off in the mud.

A few more steps brought them to a fast-running stream, where the trail ended abruptly.

'Where now?' asked Minnie. 'The footprints just stop.'

'He must have carried on upstream. Or down it.'

'Yes, but which?' said Minnie.

'I don't know. Give me the map a second.'

Amid the wooded areas on the map, Freddy could see a wriggly blue line where the stream ran. But it was impossible to tell which part of it they were at.

'So which way do we go?' Minnie glanced in both directions. The stream trickled downwards to the left, chuckling merrily over stones, while to the right it led up a rocky incline, leading back towards its source in the hills.

'I say we go right,' said Freddy.

'I knew you'd say that,' said Minnie.

'Why?'

'Because it's more difficult.'

They set off, splashing through the cold water.

'At least this way, if anybody's following *our* footprints, we can shake them off,' said Freddy.

The further uphill they went, the larger and more jagged the rocks in the stream became. They had to hold on to tussocks of grass for balance. The stones were wet and slippery so it was hard going and they often slithered over. The incline got steeper and steeper the higher they climbed, and soon the backs of their legs were aching.

After an hour's relentless trudging, Minnie suddenly grabbed Freddy's sleeve. 'Hold on, I think I saw something,' she said.

She splashed back a few steps and stared down to where a pinkish object was caught spinning in an eddy of fast-moving water.

'There!'

She peered closer, then jumped back in disgust. 'Eugh!'

'What is it?'

'It's a – a – a finger!'

Summoning their courage, they bent down to look.

Minnie let out a sigh of relief. 'It's not human. It's from Dad Droid!' She held up the severed dripping finger, still in its fleshy rubber coating. Wires were sticking from the end, where it had been ripped out.

'He must have caught it on one of these rocks,' said Freddy.

'Proves we're going in the right direction anyway,' said Minnie, pocketing the finger.

A few minutes later the stream ran under

a small road bridge and they stopped in the brickwork arch to rest. They were light-headed from not having eaten since the day before. Minnie searched her bag and found some Monkey's Tangy Nibble-tails she'd tucked away for emergencies, which they had for breakfast.

While they were busy munching the sour-dusted jellies, they heard the roar of approaching engines and the bridge shook as several vehicles screeched to a halt above. There was the sound of doors opening and people getting out, followed by raised voices. Minnie gestured to Freddy to creep further into the shadows.

'You almost crashed into me, you idiot!' came a voice from above.

'That's my father,' Minnie whispered.

'You ridiculous little man! You veered right across the road,' snapped another voice.

'That's Miss Dribb!' said Freddy.

They kept very still.

'Have you seen those children anywhere?' Mr Dribb asked sharply.

'Of course not,' said Minnie's mother. 'Do you think we're driving round this stupid wood for fun?'

'It's the boy *we* want,' said Miss Dribb. 'That's what this net's for. It's boy-sized.'

'You're welcome to him. He's nothing but a troublemaker,' said Minnie's dad. 'I've reported him to the police for kidnapping my daughter.'

There was the sound of fierce scribbling. 'I'm writing that down!' said Miss Dribb, with relish. '*Kidnapper.*'

'I didn't *kidnap* you!' Freddy whispered to Minnie.

'I know. How insulting. I'm not a "kid"!' said Minnie, with disgust.

They crept to the edge of the tunnel and peered out. The grey P.O.O.F.A.C.E. van was parked at a rakish angle on the hump of the bridge with Mr and Mrs Carstairs's car in front of it. The doors of both vehicles were wide

open and Minnie's parents and the Dribbs were arguing by the roadside.

As they crawled back under the bridge to hide, Freddy caught sight of a movement behind a nearby tree. It looked like a foot in a yellow boot. There was a flash of a tan-coloured shoe from the other side.

Odd shoes…

Freddy prodded Minnie excitedly. 'It's Dad Droid!'

Even as they looked, they saw the droid peering from behind the tree. They waved their arms frantically to get its attention but it didn't see them.

The argument on the bridge had begun to escalate. Miss Dribb now had hold of Mrs Carstairs's handbag and was pulling on it. Mr Dribb was swiping at Minnie's dad with his net. 'How dare you call my wife an ignoramus!' Mr Carstairs was saying, grabbing at the net.

'Let go of that at once, it's government property!' Mr Dribb barked back.

Minnie's dad dragged Mr Dribb away from the van by the net. The women followed, tussling with Mrs Carstairs's bag.

Seizing the chance, Dad Droid slipped from its hiding place and ran across to the Dribbs' van.

'Look!' cried Miss Dribb. 'It's the boy's father! We've found them!'

Dad Droid's trousers were ripped, revealing parts of its metal limbs and circuitry.

'That's not his father,' said Mr Carstairs, 'it's some sort of robot! What's going on?'

'A robot?' said Mr Dribb indignantly.

'That explains everything!' said Miss Dribb, thinking back to the confusion at Freddy's house. 'The boy tricked us! Quick, Mr Dribb! The net!'

As the children looked on, they saw Dad Droid jump in the front seat of the van.

'What's he doing?' said Minnie.

'I don't know. But come on, before he gets away.'

Before anyone could stop them, the children ran out from under the bridge and leapt in beside the droid. Dad Droid turned the key in the ignition. The engine roared to life. It slammed its foot down on the accelerator. Being a metal foot, this meant the van swerved off at incredible speed.

As they skidded past the Carstairses car and sped down the road, the children looked back to see Miss Dribb running after them, shaking her fist. Then she tripped over a stone, falling flat on her face in the mud.

They burst out laughing. 'Serves her right!'

Freddy looked at Dad Droid. Apart from a missing finger, and some wisps of smoke rising from its wet feet, it seemed unharmed.

'Where have you been?' he said angrily. 'Why did you just walk off?'

Dad Droid said nothing. Its eyes were glazed over, like

they'd been the night before, its mind circuits fixed on something.

'Slow down!' said Minnie, as the van screeched round a corner. The road through the woods was very old and full of potholes, so they bucked and shuddered crazily as they sped along.

'I didn't know he could drive,' said Minnie.

At that moment they skidded off the tarmac and began hurtling through trees at breakneck speed.

'It can't!' said Freddy.

He grabbed Dad Droid's arms, trying to prise its hands off the wheel, but its grip was too strong. The van raced between tree trunks, sending puddles splashing and leaves flying in its wake. Branches thrashed against the bodywork and scraped the windows.

'Where are you taking us?' Freddy demanded. His voice was wobbly from the juddering vehicle. 'TALK TO ME, YOU PIECE OF TIN!'

But Dad Droid just kept driving, calculating the precise distances between trees by using a grid system in its brain processor. They were heading steadily upwards through the tree-lined slopes.

'He seems to know where he's going,' Minnie shouted over the roar of the engine.

'Yes, but where's that?' Freddy shouted back.

As they sped up an increasingly steep incline, pens and objects on the dashboard showered back at them. Freddy and Minnie were pressed back in their seats like astronauts about to take off.

'Please, Dad Droid, listen to me. It's not safe. We have to stop,' Minnie pleaded.

The van shot from the cover of the trees onto flatter ground and hit a patch of black mud.

'Wooooooah!'

The children clung on as it skidded out of control, spinning in a circle with a deafening screech of brakes. Dad Droid tried to force the steering wheel against the momentum, its mind flashing impossibly fast through information on road safety from page 17 of *The Highway Code* in Freddy's house.

The terrifying spin seemed to go on forever till, with a massive clunk, they came to a halt and the van lurched forward, the engine cutting out.

All was suddenly quiet.

Minnie opened her eyes, which she had been clenching shut, and stared out. Then wished she hadn't. They were balanced on the edge of a massive drop. The countryside stretched out miles below, the fields like tiny squares on a model railway. The van's front wheels were dangling in mid-air, the whole vehicle teetering dangerously.

'Don't move!' she said.

Freddy was on the floor, clutching on. 'Why not?' he said, trying to stand.

The van lurched forward with a creak.

'Because *that'll* happen!'

Freddy got a glimpse of the yawning drop below and let out a hysterical laugh. He was terrified of heights.

'It's – I mean – we're – ha ha ha!'

'Don't panic,' said Minnie.

Dad Droid had frozen in calculation mode, trying to compute what to do next.

'Move back, very slowly,' said Minnie, unclicking her seat belt. 'If we put all our weight in the back of the van, we might be able to swing it to safety.'

As if they were in slow motion or moving through thick soup, Freddy and Minnie began to ease their way over the back of the seats into the space behind the driver's cab. At every move, the van wobbled and the landscape below them lurched.

'Copy what I do. If we move at the same time, we might stop it rocking so much.'

Freddy nodded. He had gone very pale and could no longer speak from fear. Concentrating on Minnie and mirroring her movements like he was watching his own reflection, Freddy swung an arm and then a leg over the seats.

'Good,' said Minnie calmly. She wasn't feeling calm but she knew if she pretended to be, it would help both of them.

They eased themselves onto the metal floor behind the seats and slid carefully to the back of the van. Gradually, they felt the weight shift and the van creak gently backwards, away from the drop.

'It's working!' said Freddy. 'We're going to be all right!'

A sudden squawk at the windscreen made them look up. A crowbot had landed on the bonnet and was flapping wildly, tapping its beak on the glass.

'What's that doing here?' cried Freddy.

Timmy jumped out of Freddy's rucksack and leapt onto the dashboard, to attack. The van dipped forward again, unbalanced by the weight of the cat.

'NOOOOOO!' both children cried.

The droid was suddenly alert. In one quick movement, he wrenched the gearstick into reverse and slammed down the accelerator. Freddy and Minnie were thrown back against the rear doors of the van as, with a crunch of gears, the van slid back onto the muddy hillside to safety.

Dad Droid turned the wheel and started to speed in

the opposite direction. The crowbot gripped onto the windscreen and fluttered about, making it impossible to see out. Thinking fast, Minnie reached over and switched on the windscreen wipers. The bird was swept clumsily aside, shrieking in protest.

Now they were rising to the summit of the hill, plunging into a bank of fog. Back in their seats again, Freddy and Minnie leaned forward and looked out. Ahead, in the sickly yellow mist, loomed a familiar sight.

The factory!

They had travelled a full circle across country and were approaching it from the other side. The engine roared as Dad Droid pressed the accelerator flat to the floor, heading straight for the factory wall.

'He's going to kill us!' said Freddy, diving for the brake pedal. But Dad Droid pushed him away.

Minnie rattled the door but it was locked.

'Let us out, Dad Droid!' she demanded.

'He's not *Dad* Droid any more,' said Freddy bitterly. 'My dad would never do anything to hurt me. I thought he was my friend but he's just a heap of junk!'

The needle on the speedometer trembled into the red.

'He's gone mad! We're going to crash!' Minnie cried, trying to hold on.

'Get in the back. Lie down,' said the droid calmly.

'Do what he says!'

Freddy scooped up Timmy then pulled Minnie over

the seats into the back of the van again, where they threw themselves down, covering their heads with their hands.

Seconds later there was a deafening boom and the sound of shattering glass as the van crashed headlong through the wall into the factory. Then there was silence.

17

THE LITTLE GREEN LIGHT

As the dust settled, Freddy sat up and patted himself down to check he was unharmed. Peering out from under his jacket, Timmy's eyes bulged wide with shock.

Freddy turned as Minnie sat up next to him, adjusting her glasses, 'Are you all right?'

'I think so.'

They looked across at Dad Droid, slumped motionless over the steering wheel, covered in shards from the broken windscreen. The front of the van had caved in on impact and the engine was hissing under the buckled bonnet. Freddy forced open a crumpled door of the van and helped Minnie out, then leant back in to try and free the droid.

'Help me,' Dad Droid said.

Now it was bent forward, the children could see a green light flashing from a gash in its neck.

'What's that?' asked Freddy.

'Looks like some sort of tracking device,' said Minnie. 'He must be homing in on something.'

'That's why he brought us here!'

They stood aside as the droid slowly hauled itself out of the wreckage and began shuffling zombie-like, on its last reserves of power, down a long, winding corridor into the building.

'Come on, let's follow him!' said Freddy, helping Timmy into his rucksack.

'Wait! I don't trust him. He could be taking us straight to Wortnall.'

Freddy turned to Minnie, his eyes sparkling. 'No. He's taking me to my dad! I know it!'

He ran to catch up with the robot. Minnie had little choice but to follow.

Alarms had begun to shriek inside the factory. Red lights were flashing everywhere, alerting people to the intruders. They heard footsteps echoing down the tunnels, heading their way.

'Someone's coming! What are we going to do?' said Minnie, scanning for a place to hide. They were in a stretch of corridor with a single door in it. She tried the handle. It was locked.

Still following its signal, Dad Droid strode to the door and wrenched it off its hinges. Freddy and Minnie jumped through just in time after it, as men in overalls ran past, searching for them.

They found themselves in the courtyard at the centre of the complex, surrounded by vast metal cooling towers and chimneys. The light on the droid's neck began to pulse more intensely.

'Look. It's getting stronger,' said Freddy. 'We must be close now.' He was bubbling with excitement, convinced that at any minute he'd be reunited with his dad.

The droid led them across the courtyard to a long building made of corrugated iron, with a handwritten sign on the door saying 'WORKSHOP'.

'That's my dad's writing!' Freddy said. 'This is his workshop! I was right!'

The droid pushed aside the door and walked in. Freddy followed, thoughts racing through his mind. He imagined his dad sitting inside, working away on something, lost in thought, turning to look up at him.

He skidded to a halt in shock, taking in a hi-tech science lab with workbenches, electronics, tools and computers. Everything was blackened, the monitors shattered. Glancing up, he could see an enormous black hole where the roof had been blasted open.

His dad's workshop had been at the heart of the explosion.

Freddy felt like all the breath had been taken out of him. He slumped onto a stool, staring at the horrible black patch. He suddenly looked very pale and small.

In the corner was a machine with a platform and a small

green light on it, winking, just like the one on the homing device. A sign – 'DROID CHARGING STATION' – hung above it. The droid heaved its metal feet onto the platform and came to a standstill with a magnetic clunk.

'Of course! He was coming back to *charge* himself,' said Minnie. 'He was running out of power.'

Freddy said nothing. He had turned away.

Minnie stared up at the burnt-out roof. 'Look at this place, Freddy. If anyone was here when it exploded, they'd definitely be d—' She broke off.

Freddy stood up and faced her. 'They'd be "what"?' he demanded.

Minnie gulped. 'I was going to say they'd be dead,' she said softly, gesturing round the blackened room. 'I'm really sorry, Freddy.' She tried to take his hand but he pulled away.

'Let's get out of here,' he said in a flat voice and strode out.

*

Back in the main factory building, they emerged into a passage with the mouths of several large, rusty pipes set in the walls, curving downwards. Brown murky dust was wafting out of them, making the air hazy.

'It's over. I'm going home,' said Freddy wearily.

Minnie held onto his arm and dug her heels in to stop him.

'But if you do, the Dribbs will get you!'

'I know.'

'And what about Wortnall? He'll keep coming after you until he gets your dad's notebook!'

'Then I'll give it to him.'

He grabbed Minnie's backpack and pulled out the book.

'Think of the trouble your dad went to, to hide it!' she said.

'I don't care any more.'

Minnie stopped suddenly, sniffing the air. 'Eugh! What's that smell?'

The cabbagy whiff was familiar to Freddy at once: 'Wortnall's cigars.'

She pulled him out of sight around a corner as Mr Wortnall waddled into view on his stumpy legs, flanked by Mr Troff and Mr Peek. Although he was dwarfed by the lumbering henchmen, they cowered away from him, terrified.

'You fools!' he croaked. 'Without Bird's notebook we can never build a droid!'

Troff and Peek twitched at his every word as if lots of little arrows were being slung at them along with his spit. Wortnall's eyes flashed as he jabbed his cigar at the two men, who were muddy and worn out, having just arrived back from their all-night hunt.

'And you let the *boy* get away right under your fat noses!'

'He was very cunning, Mr Wortnall, sir,' Peek muttered.

'Cunning? A *snail* could get away from you!'

'No, no, I think we could catch a *snail*,' said Troff meekly.

'Shut up!' Mr Wortnall snapped.

'The crowbots will soon track those children down, sir, wait and see,' said Mr Peek, attempting a smile.

'Pah! I'm sick of waiting! – I'm putting you both back on toilet duty, where you belong.'

'Is *this* what you're looking for?'

Minnie did a double take from her hiding place;

Freddy had stepped out in front of Wortnall, holding up his father's notebook.

'Well, look who it is! – Er-er-er-Freddy!' Mr Wortnall shoved Troff and Peek aside and paced towards him. 'Sensible boy,' he cooed, delighted. 'I knew you'd come round in the end.'

He stepped closer, sucking on his cigar.

Under the neon lights his white face and hair looked paler than ever, like some sort of creature from a dank dark cave that never sees the light of day.

Troff and Peek chuckled, displaying rows of uneven teeth. They were ecstatic to see Freddy and the book, knowing this would save them from cleaning dirty toilets.

'After all, I paid your father to create that droid,' Wortnall purred. 'So that book belongs to me. Your father got greedy, boy. He wanted this invention for himself, to make him rich. That's why he hid it from me.'

'My dad's not greedy – I mean, he – he wasn't,' Freddy stuttered, trying not to cry. 'He wasn't interested in money. He just wanted to create amazing inventions.'

'Huh! You're just a child! What would you know?'

'I know my dad better than anyone,' said Freddy quietly, gripping the notebook tight.

'Really? Are you sure about that?'

'He was kind and amazing and brilliant!' Freddy sobbed.

Wortnall exhaled smoke right in Freddy's face, making him splutter through his tears.

From her vantage point around the corner, Minnie shook with rage. She wanted Freddy to smash Wortnall over the head with the notebook. But instead Freddy was just staring at his shoes (his *Gavins*, made by C. G. Wortnall) and looking sorry for himself.

'Give me the book,' said Mr Wortnall, his hypnotic eyes boring into Freddy's. Freddy felt like he was melting into the floor, becoming smaller and smaller. Wortnall was like all the worst teachers rolled into one, who could make you feel stupid and bad and confused all at the same time. Wortnall held out his pudgy hand. His fingers were stained yellow from tobacco.

'Give it to me,' he repeated coldly.

His spirit crushed, Freddy held out the book to him.

A smile lurked round Wortnall's toady lips. 'Good boy.'

'AAAAAAAAAGH!'

A sudden shriek filled the corridor. Minnie ran from her hiding place headlong into Freddy, rugby-tackled him and propelled both of them – along with the notebook – down one of the rusty pipes in the wall, sending Wortnall flying into Troff and Peek.

The children plunged into darkness.

'AAAAAAAAAAAGH!'

Behind them they heard cursing as the men tried to jump after them. But the opening was too narrow.

The pipe curved round, bumping the children back and forth off its slimy walls. Then it reached a long straight section. They slid down at an impossible angle, faster and faster, the skin on their faces pushed upwards as though they were on a roller coaster, till finally they shot out of an opening at the bottom and sailed through mid-air for a few seconds, before landing with a *thunk* on a bed of brown-yellow gunk.

A moment later the red notebook shot out too and bumped Freddy on the head.

'What d'you think you're doing?' he yelled at Minnie, springing up. The gunky stuff was sticking to him all over.

'Stopping you from doing the stupidest thing you've ever done,' Minnie said.

'What do you mean?'

'Giving your dad's notebook to that toad is the last thing he would have wanted!'

'It doesn't matter any more! Don't you understand – he's gone!' Freddy shouted.

There was a dull whimper from the rucksack and poor Timmy blinked out. One look at their surroundings was enough to send him diving back into the bag, leaving just his pink tail sticking out.

Freddy hauled the rucksack onto his back and looked round. They were in some sort of basement, where the dregs from the factory ended up. Choking fog, the same yellow colour as the smoke that clung to the hillside, filled the space, swirling about. The deep hum of machinery made the whole place shudder. Every now and then they felt a rush of air and heard a sickly glooping sound as more waste-stuff gushed in.

'Let's look for a way out,' said Minnie, wading through goo.

'Brilliant! Pushed down a waste pipe!' Freddy muttered. 'Thanks a lot.'

The outline of a door became visible, glowing like a rectangle of heavenly light. They headed towards it and emerged into a narrow concrete corridor illuminated by flickery strip-lights, which looked like a service tunnel. The ceiling and walls were a tangle of cables and pipes, through which they could hear liquid gurgling. The fog hovered at knee level here.

It was too cramped to walk side by side so Minnie went in front. The air was sweltering because of the hot pipes and they were soon sweaty and exhausted.

'All these tunnels look the same. It's like a maze,' said Freddy.

Minnie suddenly backed up, signalling Freddy to be quiet.

'What is it?' he whispered.

At the end of a long tunnel, they saw a hunched figure creeping by, swinging a torch. It was Wortnall.

They began to walk faster, pausing at every turn to check where he was. Three times they saw his black-clad form scuttle past. Minnie pictured the network of passages from above, thinking of their little figures moving further and further into a tangled web, pursued by Wortnall's black spider-like shape.

They rounded a corner and came to a dead end. There was a shout then a sharp, ringing clang, somewhere behind, which made them jump. Wortnall was cursing to himself and striking the pipes.

'WHERE ARE YOU, BOY?' They heard him boom. 'WHEREVER YOU ARE, I'LL FIND YOU!'

Freddy glanced over Minnie's shoulder and saw the black figure dart across the tunnel, right behind them. He pulled her down into the low-lying fog.

'We're trapped!'

Minnie scanned the blank wall ahead of them. With a yelp of excitement, she pointed to a small black square, like the entry device at the front of the factory.

'It's one of those buttons!' she said, leaping up. 'It must be a door!'

'It won't work. Not with your fingerprint. It has to be someone who works here.'

'Then it's no good,' she sighed, digging her hands in her pockets. As she did, her hand closed around the droid's severed finger from the stream.

'Freddy! Dad Droid's finger! We can use *that*!'

The finger still had its fleshy rubber coating, moulded from Bert Bird's actual hand. On the tip, they could make out a fingerprint.

Minnie reached up and pressed the droid's finger on

the square. There was a ping and the square went green. A computerised voice said: '*Fingerprint identified. Mr B. Bird. Entry permitted.*' Then the wall swung open. The children ran through into a dingy room lit by a bare bulb. As they did, a figure rose from a dirty mattress on the floor.

'Freddy?' said a familiar voice.

Freddy blinked in disbelief. 'Dad Droid?' he said, in a shaky voice.

'Who?' the figure asked, confused. 'No, Fred. It's *me*! Your *dad*!'

Freddy's heart leapt like it was on a bungee rope. He ran headlong into his father's arms and hugged him like he'd never hugged before.

Tears – this time of joy – streamed down his cheeks as he felt Bert's scratchy chin and big warm arms around him.

18

37.7778 DEGREES

Bert fixed his eyes on Freddy and Minnie in amazement. 'It's like a dream! – hold on, maybe I *am* dreaming. That's happened before.' He pinched himself to make sure. 'Ow! – No. I'm definitely awake.' He was looking very skinny and his clothes were shredded like a shipwrecked sailor's. The room was a concrete cell with nothing but a bare mattress and some old blankets. The walls had numbers and diagrams scrawled all over them, where Bert had been jotting down ideas while he was a prisoner.

'But how did you get into the cell?' he asked.

Minnie held up the droid's finger.

Bert took it, in wonder. 'Then you found the robot?'

'We didn't just *find* it, Dad, we *built* it,' said Freddy. 'We called him Dad Droid.'

Bert's mouth fell open. 'What! But how did you power it?'

'It's a long story but, basically – the cat.' He turned

round, showing Timmy sticking out of his rucksack. Timmy was so delighted to see his master that surges of electricity sparked over his whiskers.

'But what happened to *you*, Dad?' said Freddy. 'Why are you locked in here?'

'After I saw how upset you were, Freddy, I started to realise what Wortnall was really like and how blind I'd been. Then I found out what he was planning to do with the droid and I knew I had to stop him.'

'Why? What *is* he planning?'

'When I started on the project, he said he wanted to make droids to *help* people. But then I found out he actually wanted to *replace* them! Eventually, we'd end up with a town full of robots all doing exactly what Wortnall wanted, like an army, and everyone else would be driven out.'

'He's mad!' said Minnie.

'Yes! So anyway, I smuggled the droid out of the factory and blew up my workshop,' Bert continued, 'hoping Wortnall would think everything, including me, had been destroyed. But he caught me trying to escape. He's kept me down here, trying to force me to give up my secrets ever since.'

Minnie held up the red notebook. 'Don't worry. He hasn't found out anything.'

'Well done. I'm so proud of you both,' said Bert.

Freddy nodded towards the door. 'Come on. Let's get out of here.'

'You're not going anywhere,' said a voice behind them. Wortnall was in the doorway, smoke churning round him from the tunnel. He swung his blinding torch at them.

'Give me that book,' he croaked.

Minnie shook her head. 'No way, you revolting little man!'

'You might change your tune when you see this,' said Wortnall, pulling out a gun.

Bert herded the children behind him and, taking the notebook from Minnie, said: 'All right, have it.'

He threw the book across the room. It landed with a thump at Wortnall's feet.

'DAD, NO!' Freddy clung to his father.

'We've got no choice,' said Bert.

Wortnall scooped up the precious notebook, greedily.

'You've got what you wanted, Wortnall. Now let us go,' said Bert.

Mr Wortnall gave a dry chuckle. 'I don't think so.'

He backed out of the cell, still training the gun on them as he reached up to the black square to shut the door. But before he got a chance there was a clunk in the tunnel behind him. Wortnall spun round but the brown-yellow fug made it impossible to see further than a few feet. A shape was just visible, lumbering towards him.

'Is that you, Peek?' said Wortnall.

There was no reply.

'Troff? Is it you?'

The shape came closer, footsteps ringing out on the metal floor.

'No. It's me,' said a voice that sounded exactly like Freddy's father.

Wortnall's mouth dropped open. He could see Freddy's dad coming towards him down the tunnel, yet the *same man* was standing in the prison cell behind him!

Freddy glanced across at Minnie, excitedly.

Dad Droid was alive again – recharged!

Wortnall cowered in fear and confusion, glancing from Freddy's dad to the identical-looking figure, trying to make sense of what was going on.

'Who is it, Bird? Is it your twin brother?' he gabbled.

But Bert was speechless too, seeing his creation alive in front of him for the first time.

Without waiting for an explanation, Wortnall raised his gun, aimed straight at the droid's heart and fired.

'NO!' screamed Freddy.

The bullet stopped dead, trapped between two metal ribs. Dad Droid strode on towards Wortnall, unaffected. Wide-eyed, terrified, Mr Wortnall backed away, raising his gun again. But, noticing a gash in the robot's neck with circuits poking out, it finally dawned on him what he was looking at.

'So you *did* it, Bird! You *did* make your robot!' A grin spread across Wortnall's slimy lips. 'And now it's mine! – Stop where you are!' he ordered the droid. 'Listen to me!

I am your master!' He held up the notebook on which his company logo was clearly stamped. 'See this? – *C. G. Wortnall* – that's me. I paid for every nut and bolt in your body!'

Dad Droid frowned, processing this information. Now it was nearer and the fog was drifting away, the children could see it had a nasty dent in its head.

Freddy stepped forward. 'Don't listen to him, Dad Droid. My dad invented you, and Minnie and I built you! You belong to *us*!'

The droid screwed up its face, struggling to control its thoughts. Sparks spidered over its damaged head. '*I would like to buy a single ticket to Morocco*,' it stammered.

'Oh, no! It's going wrong again,' groaned Minnie.

'It must have got damaged in the crash,' said Freddy.

Bert was intrigued. 'That's one of the phrases from my *Voice-Translation System*.'

'Yes, I used it to teach the droid to speak like you,' said Freddy proudly.

Bert patted him on the back. 'Brilliant, Freddy! You've got a real inventor's mind!'

Wortnall cocked his gun at Dad Droid again. 'Turn round! Get down that tunnel. You're coming with me.'

The droid stared at the logo on the notebook, trying to compute what it should do. It *was* created out of objects this man had paid for. Therefore it *did* belong to him. Dad Droid turned on its heel and started to walk down the tunnel away from Bert and the children, its head bowed. Wortnall gave a triumphant cackle and strode after it.

They had only gone a few steps, however, when Freddy called after them: 'Wait! Dad Droid! Remember the stories on my bookshelf!'

A glint came into Dad Droid's eyes. Once again all the emotions and the colour and excitement of the tales it had read fizzed through its memory banks. The dragons and the castles and the heroes risking everything for those they loved…

'Remember our home movies!' said Freddy. 'Remember how my dad helped me and cared for me because he loves me!'

Bert shook his head. 'You're wasting your time, Freddy. It can't understand emotion. It's a machine.'

'Move, you walking trash-can!' Wortnall commanded.

But the droid stopped and began to smile, thinking of the home movies – even though they were all rather jumbled and confused in its defective memory.

All through its metallic body, a strange tingle that wasn't exactly electricity began to glow, emanating from its robotic heart.

Dad Droid turned and strode back to Freddy, pushing Wortnall aside.

'Eh? What's going on? What are you doing?' Wortnall spluttered.

The droid put its arms round Freddy so that two Berts were protecting him on either side, and squeezed him, full of what the encyclopedia had said was called 'affection'.

'Erm, that's a bit tight,' Freddy gasped, in the robot's steely hug.

'Sorry.'

'Enough of this!' Wortnall spat. 'Walk, robot! You belong to me!' He jabbed his gun at Dad Droid.

'Hand me the weapon, please. A gun is dangerous,' Dad Droid said calmly, reaching out to take it.

In a fit of rage, Wortnall stumbled backwards and squeezed the trigger. There was a deafening boom. The bullet blew a hole through one of the pipes above. There was a roar as it ignited gas inside. Flames billowed across the ceiling. Dad Droid yanked the gun from Wortnall and hurled it aside.

Before they could stop him, Wortnall pressed the black square in the wall, trapping the two children, Bert and Timmy in the cell. Then he turned and ran back into the maze of corridors, as fat clouds of orange fire puffed along the roof of the tunnel after him. Dad Droid could hear thumps and cries from inside the cell as the prisoners hammered on the door.

'Touch the black square!' came Minnie's muffled voice.

As the droid reached out to operate the door, a curtain of flames licked down, igniting its sleeve. There was just time to press the button before the flames got to his rubber skin, melting away his fleshy glove.

'Fingerprint identified. Mr B. Bird. Entry permitted.'

The cell swung open and Dad Droid's companions tumbled out as he patted himself down, putting out the flames.

'Watch out!' said Bert, pulling the children to the ground as flames roared above them.

'Which way?' said Minnie as they ran along at a crouch.

Despite being in the midst of the worst danger they had faced yet, Dad Droid remained unfazed. 'A map of the lower level is imprinted in my memory,' it said, and internally brought up a 3D layout of the floor plan they were moving along. 'Follow me, please.'

They reached a corner but had to leap back as a wall of fire wolfed towards them.

'Reassessing route,' said Dad Droid, bundling them in a different direction.

'Pretty useful in an emergency, wouldn't you say?' said Bert proudly.

They could hear deep rumbling above. The inferno was spreading through the building fast, filling the passageways with choking smoke.

'Try not to breathe it in,' said Minnie, covering her mouth.

'This way,' said Dad Droid, hurrying them on.

It was sweltering now. The crackle of flames was right behind them. Glancing back, Freddy saw a massive fireball swelling where they'd just been standing.

They came to a metal ladder set in the wall, heading upwards. Wortnall's polished shoes were just visible, disappearing on the highest rungs. Mr Troff's voice could be heard echoing from the top of the shaft: 'The factory's on fire, sir! We have to get out!'

'I know that, you fool! What do you *think* I'm doing?' Wortnall barked back. 'Help me out!'

There was a scuffle at the top of the ladder.

'No, don't take my arm! I'm going to drop it!' Wortnall shrieked.

Then something came hurtling down the shaft straight into Freddy's arms.

'THE BOOK! AAGH! NO! IT'S GONE!' Wortnall howled down at them.

'Thanks,' said Freddy, clutching the red notebook tightly. 'Back where it belongs!'

Wortnall made to climb down the ladder to get it back, but the heat of the fire wafted up into his face. With a snarl of disgust he disappeared from view and was gone.

Dad Droid lifted Bert, Minnie and Freddy onto the ladder, one by one.

'Quickly! Climb!' it said.

The rungs were so hot they were hard to hold on to.

Freddy felt needle-sharp claws digging in his back as Timmy wriggled in the rucksack. 'Hold on, Timmy! It's going to be all right – ouch!'

At the last moment, as Dad Droid leapt onto the ladder and began to climb, the fireball, which had been growing hotter and fatter as it sped down the tunnels, burst into the space below, hissing wildly and lighting up the well shaft with golden light.

'HURRY UP! WE'LL GET FRIED!' Freddy cried.

Minnie's feet were centimetres in front of him. All her muscles were aching from the effort of climbing. Sweat was pouring off her.

'I'm going as fast as I can!'

The fireball churned at the bottom of the shaft, alive with fiery tongues. The hems of Dad Droid's trousers caught alight, as the flames surged upwards. 'Temperature in service shaft approximately 37.7778 degrees Celsius and rising,' the droid reported.

Unable to contain his fear any longer, Timmy shot out of Freddy's rucksack and clung onto his head, sinking in his claws.

'Timmy, no! I can't see!'

'Miaowwwwwwwww! Miaoooowwwww!'

Freddy had to struggle on, feeling his way up the rungs.

Seconds later, they reached the top of the ladder and Bert pulled the children to safety. Dad Droid heaved the metal lid of the service shaft closed behind them. There was a boom and the floor shook as the fireball struck the lid, trying to get out. Freddy prised Timmy off his head and slung him under his arm.

'Take us to the exit, droid,' said Bert. 'Hurry!'

Dad Droid led them on.

The whole building was on fire, factory workers running in all directions, trying to get out. Alarms were shrieking, red lights flashing and the sprinkler system spraying water everywhere – but it was no match for the hungry blaze.

Near the entrance they found their way blocked by fallen pipes and chunks of concrete. A trickle of falling dust made them look up in time to see the roof splitting apart.

'LOOK OUT!'

Bert dived forward, pushing the children out of the way as a pillar crashed down. But there wasn't time to jump clear himself and it fell across his legs, trapping him.

'DAD!'

Freddy bent down and pulled at the stone column with all his might.

'Go, Freddy,' said his dad, looking up with a pale, soot-stained face, grimacing with pain. 'Get out before the whole place goes up.'

'I'm not leaving you! I just got you back!'

Freddy heaved and heaved at the pillar.

'It's no use,' said Minnie, trying to lift it too. 'It's too heavy.'

There was a terrific splitting sound as a crack splintered down the wall next to them.

'Danger increasing,' said Dad Droid. 'Please leave at once.'

Bert reached up and squeezed Freddy's hand. 'Do as it says, Freddy. Please.'

'But – but—'

'GO!' Bert shouted. 'THAT'S AN ORDER!'

Minnie pulled Freddy towards the entrance, dodging falling masonry and pools of fire.

At the open doors, they looked back and caught a last glimpse of Dad Droid inside the burning building, hugging the great pillar in its robotic arms, trying with all its might to lift it off Freddy's dad.

*

Outside had become a vision of hell: the chimneys in the middle of the factory blossoming flames, crowbots circling, cawing and screeching, their feathers on fire. They began dropping from the sky, crackling in smouldering heaps all round. Ahead of the children, people were stumbling and jumping down the hillside, running for their lives. They saw Mr Troff and Mr Peek rolling past like two great boulders.

Wortnall's shark-car emerged through the blaze at the factory entrance behind them, its grinning radiator even more demonic in the fiery light.

As it sped past them with a roar, Freddy and Minnie caught a glimpse through the open window of Wortnall hunched over the steering wheel. Unused to driving himself, he was swerving recklessly from side to side, scattering factory workers out of his path.

A moment later there was an immense explosion. A giant cauliflower-shaped cloud blasted into the sky as the factory ripped apart. The shock waves sent Freddy and Minnie tumbling down the hill in a shower of burning rubble. They came to rest in greasy scrubland, winded and bruised.

Freddy stood up, distraught, focusing on the summit of the hill. 'Dad!' he cried. 'What about my dad?'

For a moment all he could see were ruins alive with smoke and fire but as he watched, through the heat haze, he began to make out what looked like a figure clawing its way along the ground.

'There's someone there!' cried Minnie.

'Please, let it be him,' Freddy pleaded as the figure staggered to its feet, stumbling towards them. 'Let it be my dad…'

As the shape drew closer, Freddy could make out his father's features. But was it Bert or was it Dad Droid?

'FREDDY!' the figure called above the roar of flames.

Freddy ran towards him. 'Dad, is that you?'

It was only as he got closer he could see that there was no dent in the figure's head, no gash in its neck and no wires sticking out – Bert Bird collapsed on the ground next to the children, his injured legs buckling under him.

'Oh, Dad, Dad, you're all right! You're safe!' Freddy sobbed, hugging him.

'He's gone, Freddy,' Bert said, holding him tight. 'Dad Droid sacrificed himself to save me.'

It had taken all the droid's remaining strength to haul the pillar high enough for Bert to wriggle out from under it. Even as it did, the blaze finally caught up, snaking across a trail of oil spilt on the floor and rushing up the droid, from its feet upwards.

Bert caught one final glimpse of its face, which was his *own* face yet somehow wasn't like him any longer; it had become its own person with its own unique character. As the flames licked up, engulfing it, Bert had no choice but to crawl for his life.

Freddy sat back from his dad. 'I'll miss him,' he said. A lump sprang into his throat. Even if the droid *had* just been a heap of wires and steel, after all the adventures they'd been through together, it felt more like a friend.

'I'll miss him too,' said Minnie wistfully.

'Look!' said Freddy, pointing into the night sky. 'It's snowing!'

But when they held out their hands to catch the small white particles, they realised it wasn't snow at all: it was flakes of ash, the final remnants of Mr C. G. Wortnall's factory.

19

A FISH FINGER IN THE TRIFLE

At the bottom of the hill, the police were holding back a swelling crowd who'd gathered to watch the factory burn down.

Catching sight of their daughter approaching hand in hand with Bert and Freddy, Mr and Mrs Carstairs hurried from the throng towards her.

For a moment Minnie drew back, expecting them to be furious, but they were so relieved to see her safe that they hugged and kissed her and couldn't stop smiling.

'Oh, Minither-darling! Where have you been?' her mother cooed. 'Don't worry, everything's going to be all right. Although it might *not* be. You're probably in lots of trouble.'

There was an angry cry from somewhere in the crowd.

'There he is! There's the boy!'

Mr and Miss Dribb stepped forward, pushing people out of the way. Everyone went silent and turned to look at Freddy.

'We have the paperwork to take that child into care immediately!' said Miss Dribb, holding up her clipboard. 'That boy doesn't have a father!'

'Who's *he*, then?' asked an onlooker, pointing at Bert.

Mr Dribb snorted. 'Huh! That's not a man,' he said, waving his boy-sized net at Freddy's dad. 'It's a robot!'

Miss Dribb darted forward and began pulling Bert's arm frantically. 'See. This arm's artificial. It comes off!'

'Ow! Let go of me!' said Freddy's dad, shaking Miss Dribb off. 'What are you talking about? I'm not a robot!'

Miss Dribb staggered back, blushing.

The crowd all laughed at her.

'He *is*! He's got metal legs! I'll show you!' she spluttered.

Everyone was killing themselves laughing as Miss Dribb hopped about trying to pull Bert's trousers down.

'Stop it!' Mr Dribb growled, pulling her off. He could see they were defeated. 'You're making a fool of yourself!'

The Dribbs bustled off, red-faced, and were soon lost in the crowd.

'*Bye*,' Freddy called after them. 'Oh, and it *is* P.O.O.F.A.C.E., no matter what you say!'

Bert Bird turned to address the people of the town. 'There *was* a robot,' he explained. 'My son here – Freddy – built and trained it. One day he's going to be an inventor just like me!'

As a cheer rang out, a warm glow of pride passed through Freddy. Before their adventure the last thing he would have wanted was to be called an inventor, but now it felt like the biggest compliment.

He turned to Minnie. 'I couldn't have done it without you,' he said and gave her a big hug.

'A robot that looked like you, you say?' said a distinctive voice with a French accent. Miss Arbourteel slipped forward to face Bert and Freddy. 'Do you mean to say it was a *robot* that abandoned me in the restaurant?'

Bert leant down and whispered: 'What's she talking about, Freddy?'

'I'll tell you later, Dad,' he replied. He turned to Miss Arbourteel. 'Don't worry, Miss, my dad will make it up to you. He'll take you for another meal, won't you, Dad?'

'What? Oh, yes. I suppose so,' said Bert, rather flustered, a blush rising across his face.

'I will look forward to that very much,' said Miss Arbourteel, smoothing a stray curl of hair into her bun.

*

All the way back, as they walked home, the factory kept smouldering, spreading a warm glow across the rooftops of the town.

As Freddy led his dad up the path, he stopped short. The front door was still hanging off its hinges, where it had been kicked in.

'Oh, I forgot to tell you, Dad, Wortnall's thugs have wrecked the house.'

'Have they?' Bert looked round at the devastation without surprise, used to seeing his mess everywhere. 'It looks exactly how I left it.'

There was a muffled miaow from Freddy's rucksack. 'Poor Timmy!' Freddy undid his rucksack and the cat jumped out, delighted to be home at last. 'You're safe now,' he said.

'Ah, and my notebook,' Bert declared, spying a red corner poking out. He pulled it from the bag and placed it on the table. 'Good. We'll be needing that.'

'What for?' asked Freddy.

'To make the next droid, of course.'

'What?'

'We'll build it together this time, Freddy. You saw how Dad Droid saved me from the fire. We'll make droids that can go into places where it isn't safe for humans to go, just like *he* did. Yes... Rescue Droids!'

He leant forward, examining the front of the notebook. 'Pass me that pen, would you?' He began to scribble on the cover.

*

Not long after the factory had burnt down and Mr Wortnall had disappeared, all the *You-Shoes* machines went out of service. Mr Carstairs began to sell normal shoes again and made a small fortune, as he was the only shoe salesman to hold on to all his stock.

Because of this, the Carstairs didn't have to sell their house after all, so Minnie could still wave across to Freddy from her room next door (or talk to him, of course, using the *Ear to Ear* device).

*

One night, while his dad was sitting listening to Uncle Oony's Orchestra in the front room, Freddy caught sight of the red notebook on a shelf. Taking it down, he noticed Bert had scribbled out the Wortnall logo on the cover and in its place instead, in big fancy letters, he had written:

'Bert Bird & Son: Droidmakers'

Under it he'd added:

'(And Minnie too!)'

That small yet formidable person would be essential in all the new inventions they might make. *Doopy-doopy-do, doopy-do, doopy-do,* went the orchestra, while Uncle Oony sang in his unmistakable raspy voice through the sound horns in the corners:

Da Monkey's in me barf again,
It's really hard to cope!
It's dancing on me hot tap
It's nibbling me soap!

Freddy looked up and saw Timmy beaming down at him, circling the chandelier in his new, improved *Pet-to-Vet* cat-airship, chasing a nice fat moth. Below, his dad was dipping a fish finger in the rhubarb trifle and tapping his foot to the music.

Freddy smiled.

Everything was back to normal.

The End

ACKNOWLEDGEMENTS

We would like to thank Mathew Clayton, Anna Simpson, Imogen Denny, Georgia Odd and the rest of the team at Unbound for their great encouragement and enthusiasm, Lola Bubbosh for starting the ball rolling, and all the friends, family and supporters who have helped us get the book into print. Thanks also to Amanda Davis and Gordon Wise at Curtis Brown.

A NOTE ON THE AUTHORS

Chris Bran and Justin Chubb are writers and comedians, originally from the Channel Islands, and friends since school. They are best known for creating and starring in the series *This is Jinsy* for Sky Atlantic, which was nominated for both a Rose d'Or and a British Comedy Award.

Unbound is the world's first crowdfunding publisher, established in 2011.

We believe that wonderful things can happen when you clear a path for people who share a passion. That's why we've built a platform that brings together readers and authors to crowdfund books they believe in – and give fresh ideas that don't fit the traditional mould the chance they deserve.

This book is in your hands because readers made it possible. Everyone who pledged their support is listed below. Join them by visiting unbound.com and supporting a book today.

Yasmina Al-Shammas
Anthony Albright
Jon Allbon
Lucy Allen
Mark Allison
Andrew & Michelle
 Chalet 34
Sarah Angliss
Richard Atkinson
Claire Bailey
Tom Bainton
James Banbury
JL Banks
Nate and Alec Banner
Philip Barham
Sonny Barnett
Richard Bazin
Katy Beaulieu
Trace Beaulieu
Helen Bebbington

Kasper Behrendt
Julian Benton
Michael Betti
Etta Bingham
Alex Birtwisle
Heather Blake
Bridget Bluck
Pablo Bollansée
Leo Bonnafous
Wendy Bosberry-Scott
Lee Bradshaw
Gillian Bran
Janet & Tony Bran
Tim Bran
Tony Bridgeman
Chris Brock
Steph Burke
Valley Burke
Debbie Butler
Moira Butterfield
Hannah Butters
Andrew Camsell
Nikki Canning
Caroline Cantor
Chris Carey
Sarah Carratt
Julie Carre
Lucy Carter
Angela Casey
Lucy Chaplin
Julian Chappell
Charlotte Clark
Mathew Clayton
James Cleal
Mark Clendenning
Diane Cockerham
Tony Cockerham
Jack Cocking
Marc Cohen
Barrie Cooper
Indigo P Cooper
James Coppen
Simon Craddock
Sophia Craddock
John Crawford
Peter Creed
Julia Crofts
Sarah Crowther
Emma David
Nadine Davidson
Rachel Davies
Sue Davies
Tref Davies
David Dawson

John de Garis
AJ de Montjoie
James Dean
Jo Delbridge
Gary Dennis
Chris Devaney
Michael Dewar
Andy Dixon
Lucy Dodds
Sharon Dominey
Karen Donlon
Peter Dorsett
Tim Downie
Claire Durbar
Ruth Dye
Felix and Flynn East
Julie Edmunds
Janine Edwards
Suzanne English
Conrad Evans
Lee Exelby
Ninette Finch
Glory Fink
Steve Foote
Jennifer Ford
Andrew Fothergill
Dave Fox
Keith Franklin
Ben Freeman
Paul W Frick
Oral R. Friend
Andie Fuller
Ruth Gardner
Peter Gleeson
Claire Golding
Ed Golding
Sara Graham
Jane Gregory
David Grewcock
Stephen Grier
Mandy Griffin
Julie Hadley
Evelyn Hall
Jonathan Hall
Lord Pat Harkin & Lady Jan Clarke
Damian Hasenrader
Jeffrey Hayday
Ciorstaidh Hayward Trevarthen
Theophilus Heliotrope
Melissa Henderson
Thomas Hescott
Niall Hingston

Colette Hobbs
Sam Holloway
Emma Holohan
Kev Hopgood
Jeff Horne
Glen Horsley
Robert Howells
Rebecca Hubbard
Scott Hubbard
Jason Hutchinson
George Stanley Irving
Stewart Ivins
Daniel James
Ben Jones
Carol Jones
Stuart Kearns
Donna Kehoe
Gerard Kehoe
Matthew Kendall
Emma Kennedy
Roel Ketelaars
Dan Kieran
Sarah Kinmond
Liz Koe
Kluane LaBelle
Andy Lakin-Hall
Eliza Lamb
Marek Larwood
Zanna T. Laws
Susan Leiska
Tim LeRoy
Terry Livermore
Laura Lorhan
Shayne Lynch
Lou MacDonald
Jane Macintyre
Estelle Mageean
Anna Malpas
Neil Malpas
Karanasou Maria
Emma Marks
Adrienne Marlow
Nick Martin
Pip Mason
Nicole Matheus
Kate Mawby
Rod McDonald
Guy McIndoe
John McLean
Richard McLeod
Theresa McManus
Monty McMonagle
Kes Mcsheffrey
Jim Mineweaser

Leo Mirani
John Mitchinson
Henry Moody-Stuart
Felicity Morgan
Kim Morgan
Eric Morin
Tricia Moynihan
Deborah E.A. Murphy
Carlo Navato
Andrew Neal
Karen Nicholson
Sheryl Nicklin
Sarah Nixey
Elena Oliva
Julie Oliver
Kay Oxenham
Chris & Juliet Pagel
Lorraine Pannett
Heather Park
Ed Parker
Jim Parkyn
Anna Parrack
Hannah Parry-Payne
Lawrence Peachey
Mark Pearson
Jessica Pelling
Caroline Penfold
Malin Pennell
Lucy Pickering
Sophie Pickles
Elizabeth Pollard
Justin Pollard
Daisy Popham
Mary Popo
Sarah Popplestone
John Powell
Ian Pratt
Sean Raffey
Chris Ramsay
Joe Randall-Cutler
Julian Ransom
Jason Reid
Matthew Revell
Kevin Rhodes
John Rice
Hannah Richards
Angela Riches-Heed
Graham & Lindy Robertson
Alice & Thomas Robinson
Charmian Round
Vanessa Rouse
Mike Rowland
Sarah Rudiger
Ida Runberg

Sue Ryan
Jamie Sage
Jane Sales
Lauren Saunders
Claire Savage
Jenny Schwarz
Mark & Liza Scott
Nicola Scott
Nikki Scrivener
Jack Seale
Maria Sergunina
Adrian Seymour
Nur Sezgi Vurdem
Laurence Shapiro
Kiren Shoman
Matt Sims
Gavin Skipsey
Kirsty Slattery
Annie Smith
Maggie Smith
Pamela Smith
Pauline Smith
Lili Soh
Christina Stanton
Jaine Stanway
Nigel and Lisa Steggel
Mia Stevens
Alexis Strum
Simona Style
Mark Sweetland
Tracy Taft-Myers
Melanie Taylor
David Thomas
E R Thompson
Hope Toogood
Karen Trethewey
Phil Trouteaud
Amy Tucker
Andy Tucker
Angela Tucker
Nigel Turner. Jinsy praise him.
Csilla Erika Varga (Csinszka)
Jem Vaudrey
Mark Vent
Katy Waddle
Tricia Wain
Scott Wallace
Eoin Walsh
Gail Ward
Kelly Watson
Fiona and John Watt
Dr Hefina Jane Weaver

Claire Welch
B.J. West
Paul Wheatley
Daniel Whitehead
Chloe Whitmore
Ben Whitney
Ross Whittaker
Angie Wilkins
Bradley Williams
Mike Williams
Zoë-Elise Williamson
Des Willie
Jack Wise
Elizabeth Woodhouse
Helen Wrigglesworth
Marina Young